The Cure for the Curse

WhoooDoo Mysteries
A division of

Treble Heart Books
1284 Overlook Dr.
Sierra Vista, AZ 85635-5512
http://www.trebleheartbooks.com

Printed and Published in the U.S.A.

ISBN: 1-932695-41-9

Thank you for choosing a
WhoooDoo Mysteries
Vampire Selection

The Cure for the Curse
by
Patrick Vaughn

WhoooDoo Mysteries

A division of

Treble Heart Books

Dedication

For Sammy, who never stopped believing in me.

Prologue

"**R**ichard, help me!"

Warrenna Dennison lifted her head from the pillow. "Mom?"

She listened through the rain, but there was no answer, just the familiar creak of the front door swinging open and then a *clang* as it struck the wall.

But then she heard a voice: "Renna? Oh, no..." The words were gasped. "Where are you?"

Warrenna jumped from her bed. "I'm coming, mom!"

She darted down the stairs, into the hallway, where a stiff breeze rattled the frames of her mother's oil paintings.

Lightning flashed through the open door, illuminating Alexandria's slumped form. Her right hand gripped the doorknob above her head, but her left arm hung close to her side with the elbow turned in at an odd angle. Her rain-soaked dark hair clung to her face, and her pants were torn and spattered with mud.

Warrenna ran to her, shouting, "Mom, what's wrong?" But she stopped when she saw the blood.

It saturated her mother's white blouse, like a dozen red roses crushed into silk. Warrenna couldn't be sure where the bloodstains ended and the mud began.

"Renna," Alexandria wheezed, "get your father."

Rain tickled Warrenna's ears as she stared at her mother's dripping figure. "Oh, God, Mom, you're bleeding! You have to get to a hospital. I'll get the car."

Alexandria shook her head and grimaced. "I'll be fine. Just get your father."

Warrenna finally nodded and tore her gaze from the blood. But as she turned to find Richard, he strode past her to close the front door. He calmly helped his wife onto the carpet of the TV room.

"We have to go, Richard," Alexandria murmured. "I'm sorry. I couldn't stop it."

Richard nodded, his face pale. "Did you hurt anyone?"

"No." She looked away. "But I was *seen*."

He closed his eyes, but only for a moment. "It'll be okay," he whispered, and turned his attention to her injured arm. "Warrenna, go to your room and get your emergency bag."

Warrenna squinted. "My bag? But all I have in there are clothes."

"Renna!"

Richard turned around and gripped her shoulders, his sunken hazel eyes flashing. "You have one minute to pack your things, and then we leave."

"Leave?" she sputtered, fighting a sob. "Again? But why?"

"We'll explain in the car," Alexandria said. She nodded to Richard, who gave her injured arm a hard yank. Her elbow crunched into place, and she yelped from the pain. "Go, Renna." she grunted. "There isn't any time."

Bile burned Warrenna's throat as she stumbled back to her room. She yanked the drawers from her dresser, shuffling through the silly socks Melissa gave her and the shell necklace she bought at the mall with Deni. But she barely noticed any of her beloved trinkets. It was like she had never seen her room before, never seen any of her favorite things. How could she possibly choose?

She was grabbing an armful of shirts when she remembered that foggy morning three years ago, the last time her family abandoned a house on little notice.

Her mother's explanations were hardly illuminating. "It's no longer safe for us here," and "The bad people are looking for us, so we have to leave," was all Alexandria would say.

Back then, Warrenna didn't care that they were suddenly leaving town. She didn't make any friends in the year they stayed in San Francisco, and she never really liked how crowded the city felt. But this little town in Washington State was different. Melissa, Deni and Corbett accepted her as soon as she arrived in Bellingham. She felt at home somewhere for the first time. How could she leave?

She tried to tell herself this was just a bizarre hit-the-road exercise. But when she remembered the sound her mother's arm made, she knew this was no emergency drill

One minute later, Warrenna stood in the garage with her emergency bag of clothes in one hand and her travel portfolio, crammed to bursting with sketches and paintings, under her other arm. There were a hundred other things she wanted to take, but that was all she could carry.

After another minute, Warrenna and her parents were in their Volvo, racing down Interstate 5 while the rain pounded every inch of the car's black paint. Numb with grief, anger and worry, Warrenna could only listen to her parents' rushed words.

"We'll go to the old place in Bascomville," Richard said as he maneuvered the car through traffic. "No one will look for us there."

Alexandria nodded and began unbuttoning her bloodstained blouse with her good arm. "Yes, we can't risk bringing attention to Maldecido right away. We'll be safe in Bascomville." She raised her voice. "Settle in for a long trip, hon."

Warrenna's heart lurched. She had never heard of any place called "Maldecido" or "Bascomville," but she was certain there weren't any towns in Washington with those names. They were really leaving, and they weren't coming back. Melissa and Deni would never know where she went, or even why she left. And Corbett would never know how she really felt about him.

"Could one of you please tell me why we're leaving?" she blurted. "Or even what happened back there?"

Alexandria looked to Richard, but he looked away, out of the car window.

"I was in an accident on the 202, Renna," she said. Her voice sounded tired as she peeled the blood-sticky garment off her shoulders and pulled on a dark t-shirt. "It was a bad wreck, seven or eight cars. I went to check on one of the other drivers. He had a wound in his chest. He was bleeding pretty badly."

Alexandria trailed off, closing her eyes and bowing her head. Rain rattled against the roof. The wipers swished water from the windshield. A thunderclap boomed somewhere behind them.

When Warrenna finally spoke, her voice was nearly inaudible. "That's horrible," she said, the tears starting down her cheeks. "But I don't see why we have to leave town and all the friends I'd finally found."

Richard thumped the dashboard with his fist. "Damn it, Alex, we should have told her sooner."

"No," Alexandria said, her voice firm. "The less Renna knew, the safer she was."

He sighed. "I guess it doesn't matter now."

"*What* doesn't matter?" Warrenna yelled. "What's going *on*?"

Warrenna saw her father glance at her in the rearview mirror. His face was pale and drawn, like her mother's, and Warrenna imagined that her own face looked much the same.

"Smelling all that fresh blood made your mother change," Richard said at last. "Someone saw her other form, and so we have to go."

Warrenna sniffled. "What do you mean, 'other form'?"

Richard flipped on the Volvo's overhead light, then pointed to Alexandria. "*This* form."

Alexandria turned around and opened her eyes. Her irises pulsed with scarlet. The pupils were thin slits of black. Her lips curled back, revealing a set of glistening two-inch fangs. Growling wheezes escaped her mouth, like an angry, panting dog.

"Listen very carefully, Renna," Richard said. "There's something you need to know about your mother and me."

Lightning arced across the chalkboard-black sky.

"And about yourself."

Chapter I

The poison blurred his vision, but he could still see his destination in the orange tint of the clouds, and in the mountain-size shadows cast by each pebble. Home was just a few strides away.

The woman was still with him; her small hand held his arm to catch him if he stumbled. But she didn't try to pull him along with her. She knew he wanted to reach the sunset on his own, to at least walk this final stretch without aid.

He glanced at her. He couldn't make out the fine details of her face anymore, but her shallow breaths told him that tears probably streaked down her bronze cheeks. He smiled through the burning in his chest. "Thank you."

More than she knew, more than he could ever say, he would miss her.

But that was all right. They would see each other again. Of that, he was certain.

Suddenly the burning stopped. The flames licking his lungs became icicles numbing his chest and shoulders.

Another step and the dusty ground ended, dropping to dark,

reddish shadow. A warm breeze caressed the red feather in his thick hair, then faded to stillness.

He prayed that the Sky-God would give him a moment of clear sight so that he could take in the marvelous work the Divine had done to the horizon.

The sun was sinking into the desert, throwing fiery slashes of orange across the sky over his head. As they drew closer to him, those slashes darkened to dull red, then purple, then were finally consumed by the indigo of twilight. The distant mountains glowed orange, like dying embers of some massive campfire.

He watched the Sky-God's art for a few breaths, and then the darkness closed in from each side. It was time to go, but he would not let the poison take him.

His numb fingers found the knife at his belt, and his ears filled with the rushing of a thousand flooded rivers.

He plunged the knife into his heart. The ice shattered, and silence consumed the land.

Thomas Gelbaugh woke gasping, his fist held to his chest. His heart pounded for a few seconds, but then he felt the sheet balled in his hand and the pressure of the springs in the mattress beneath him. He quickly touched his chest. *No wound.* He took a deep breath and rubbed his eyes.

The room was dark except for the red glow of the digital clock by the bed: 6:14, sixteen minutes before his alarm would go off. He turned on the lamp, rolled out of bed and stumbled to the chair at his small desk. A notebook rested front and center. After a jaw-cracking yawn, Thomas picked up a pen and wrote.

The details of the dream came without effort. He described the sunset, the warrior, the fire in his chest that froze to ice, the woman, her sorrow, his peace. He stared at the blank wall as his pen moved across the page almost on its own.

Soon the alarm buzzed its annoying call, and Thomas reluctantly put down the pen and clicked the switch to stop the whining.

He glanced at the calendar: another Monday. That left just ten more Mondays until high school was over.

I've got to savor this day, even if it's a Monday.

He grabbed the day's clothes from a pile on the floor and stumbled to the shower.

"Hey, B."

"Whattup, Tom." Brendan rubbed the dark stubble on the side of his golden-brown head and groaned.

"You don't look so good."

"I don't feel so good," Brendan replied. "Janey kept me on the phone all night." He shook his head as he rubbed a coffee-colored eye. "I swear that girl's trying to kill me."

"Dude, I warned you about her," Corwyn said as he took his seat behind Brendan. He absently pulled his silver cross out from under his black t-shirt and let the symbol rest on his chest. Then he nodded at Thomas. "Hey Tom, didn't I say that *chica's* a freak? She'll never get enough of you, if you know what I'm sayin'."

Thomas grinned. "Lucky for B we don't have practice today."

"No joke," Brendan mumbled. "I don't think I could get the ball above my head today, let alone drain any shots."

"So it'd be like any other practice."

Brendan slowly swung an open hand at Corwyn's spiky, bleached-blond hair.

"Ay, watch the 'do, man!"

Just then, Thomas caught sight of Mariah's bright blue eyes as she strolled down the aisle toward the seat in front of him. He quickly smoothed his short hair.

Brendan saw the look on his friend's face, so he cleared his throat and announced, "Speaking of girls trying to kill us."

Thomas shoved Brendan's shoulder. Mariah shook her head. "Boys, boys," she said. "Fighting over me again?"

"Yeah, sorta," Thomas replied. "B here says you remind him of Christina Aguilera, but I say you're more of a Charlize Theron kinda girl."

Mariah raised her left eyebrow. "Is that so?"

"Yeah," Thomas repeated before Brendan could say anything. "You're way too classy to be Christina, and you keep your hair short like Charlize. Plus there's obviously a lot going on behind those blue eyes. So yeah, Charlize seems about right."

Brendan rolled his eyes, and Corwyn snorted, but Thomas ignored them.

Mariah smiled and affected an English accent: "Flattery will get you everywhere, Mister Gelbaugh."

Thomas winked, then looked to the head of the class as Mrs. Hayes stood from her desk. "Okay, class, settle down. Let's see if we can learn something today." She began her lecture, and Thomas's flirting seamlessly shifted to note-passing.

At first, the notes related to the class. They agreed that D.H. Lawrence had serious issues with his mother. But it wasn't long before the gossip began.

Can you BELIEVE that skirt Bethany was wearing Saturday night? Mariah's note read. *She must have been freezing. Do guys really like that?*

We actually prefer pants, Thomas wrote. *Everybody stares when guys wear skirts. (Or so I've been told).*

Halfway through the period, Mrs. Hayes asked Thomas to pass a worksheet out to the class. At the last row of desks, his hand brushed a girl's sleeve as he handed her the stack of paper. "Sorry," he said, and glanced at her face.

He recognized the gun-metal-gray eyes of the new girl. She'd been in the class for about a month, and after her first day, he'd never given her a second thought. He couldn't remember her name, or ever hearing her voice.

A cold, hard feeling developed in Thomas's stomach as he looked at the pale girl's face. It felt like he somehow swallowed a bowling ball, and the heavy weight was pulling him to the floor.

The feeling reminded him of when his best friend Steven moved away in fourth grade. Or when Eight-Ball, his cocker spaniel puppy, ran away a year later. But this feeling was even worse.

"Did you need something?" the girl whispered.

Her straight auburn hair was short, but it still managed to hang over one of her strange eyes. She blinked like he just woke her up.

Thomas wondered how long he'd stared at her. "Sorry," he said again, and shuffled back to his desk. The bowling ball in his stomach vanished after a couple of steps, but his eyes burned and his breath was reluctant.

Mariah passed him a note. *Are you all right?*

Thomas took a deep breath and rubbed his eyes like he was waking from a particularly troubling dream. *I don't know*, he scribbled. *I feel a little weird.*

You look like my cousin Chrissy did when I said goodbye to her this weekend.

Thomas was eager to think about something other than how awful he felt. *How's that new foster family working out for her?*

Not great. They've got five other adopted kids, and it seems like Chrissy gets lost in the shuffle.

At least she gets some special attention from her devoted cousin Mariah, right?

Yeah, I do what I can. But I can't believe my mother won't let her live with us.

Their written conversation turned to the familiar topic

of Mariah's mother. After a few minutes, Thomas felt like himself again.

The bell rang, and the roomful of students stood to go. Thomas looked at his friends and said, "Hey, I gotta talk to Miz H for a sec."

Mariah flashed him a smile that made him warm all over. "See you later, Tommy."

Brendan yawned. "See you lunch, Tom."

"See ya, Tommy-Gun." As he spoke, Corwyn shoved Brendan toward the door. "Dude, the day's half-over, you can wake up now."

Thomas approached Mrs. Hayes, who sat at her desk reading some papers. "Do you have a sec, ma'am?"

She looked up and smiled at him over her reading glasses. "Sure, Tom. You probably want to know if I had a chance to read your entry in the short story contest."

He smiled and his face grew hot. "Right on as usual, ma'am."

She fished through a large bag at her feet, drew out the manuscript and began looking through it. "Let's see. Yes. Your descriptions, as I've come to expect, are amazing, Tom. You were patient in describing everything—the cool night, the stars, the forest, the horse, how the man's distress affected his riding." She looked up at him, her eyes crinkling. "I was right there with him. And you kept this romantic, dreamy tone. I loved it."

Thomas smiled. Maybe the story was as good as he thought. "But."

His smile disappeared as she continued. "You didn't establish any kind of context, Tom. You don't give the reader any chance to find out why the man and woman are in the forest, or how he got his wound, or why they feel so strongly about each other. You didn't even give them names."

She smiled at Thomas's frown and touched his arm. "The sensory information is really wonderful, but a short story isn't a scene cut out of a novel. It has to belong to itself."

Mrs. Hayes handed Thomas the manuscript. "It wouldn't take very much to make this story good enough to win the contest. Just sprinkle in some history. Have the characters say something that reveals some context. You know them best. Find something they would naturally do to show the reader a little more about the situation. And give them names. Everybody has names, Thomas."

Thomas nodded and gnawed on the inside of his cheek. "Yeah, I guess everybody does. Deadline's Friday, huh?"

Mrs. Hayes's round cheeks flushed. "You can do this, Tom. You know you have it in you. You've got talent, more than anyone I've ever taught. That's why I hold you to a higher standard."

"That's really nice of you to say, Mrs. H." He turned to go.

"Tom?"

He didn't want to, but he turned around.

"Can I ask how you got this idea?"

He shrugged. "Just kinda came to me."

As he meandered to his locker, Thomas kept chewing the inside of his cheek. "Wounded Rider" was the best story he had ever written. He was sure of it. But Mrs. Hayes said it needed context, and none of his dreams ever had any context. That meant he'd have to come up with it on his own. That sounded a lot harder than just cleaning up a journal entry.

He was just as certain that whatever he added would be terrible. It would be untrue to the dream, and so it would ring hollow. So what could he do?

The hard, sinking feeling returned to his stomach. *C'mon, it's not that bad. I'll think up some back story. That weird feeling I got from the new girl just has me a little gloomy, that's all.*

He frowned. *But why did she affect me at all?*

Thomas shrugged his shoulders and headed to his locker to get his biology book.

"Very funny."

Brendan rebounded Thomas's third straight free throw. "The point of HORSE is to make a bunch of *different* shots," Brendan said.

Thomas grinned. "Man, you gotta get better if guys like Crittendon are gonna foul you all game." He released his shot, which rattled around the rim and fell out. "Crap. Now I'm a HO."

"I was gonna say something about those skanky habits."

"One crack about Mariah and I'll kick your ass."

Brendan laughed. "Chicks, man." He made a reverse lay-up. "Can't live with 'em, can't get laid without 'em."

Pinprick stars dusted the clear black sky, and the crisp desert air cooled the boys' lungs as they chased the basketball around. Thomas wondered how many hundreds of nights they'd played in Brendan's driveway, how many times they'd talked about girls, or movies, or rock groups as they dove to keep the ball out of the street.

He grinned at his friend. "Hard to believe you're the same gangly kid that used to bounce a basketball all the way to and from elementary school, man." He repeated Brendan's shot, and the ball swished through the net.

"Yeah, and you're the same kid with a strange dream-story for every single walk."

"Yeah, I was a real weirdo. You know," Thomas said as he rebounded Brendan's baseline shot, "I'm really going to miss this."

"Dude, I'm tellin' ya—come with me to UC-Santa Barbara. You could walk on. You know the game and you work hard in practice. Any coach would love to have you on his team."

Thomas shrugged. "Yeah, but there'll be other five-foot-nine guys trying to walk on. Only they'll be faster, and have a better three-point shot. And they'll have actually started on their high school teams."

Thomas bricked a hook shot.

"You should give yourself more credit," Brendan said, watching. "You're a great team player."

"Yeah, maybe. But we don't have the dough to pay for out-of-state tuition for a school in Cali. And I doubt Santa Barbara has plans to offer me a scholarship. Southern Arizona's about the only place I can afford to go."

Brendan didn't say anything as he banked in a close-range shot. He tapped the ball to Thomas, but Thomas flipped it back to him. "I'm outta here. I got some stuff to finish up. I'll see ya tomorrow."

"All right. See ya, man."

"Get some sleep!" Thomas called from the street.

By the time the '86 Escort's engine turned over, Thomas's fake smile was gone. As he drove home, he remembered riding his bicycle down the same dark streets when he was younger. It was hard to believe that in a few months they would both be gone, Brendan to Southern California, Thomas to nearby Maldecido.

I guess that's just what happens. We all move away from home, leave one life and all the people in it as we start another.

He parked his car and stared up at the streetlight that stood outside his house. The light had never changed. It had just shone, every night, guiding him home from Brendan's house for years.

How can everybody be so okay with this? How can I be the only one that feels so lost?

Thomas's throat tightened up and his heart sank into his stomach. The feeling reminded him of English class, and that girl with the odd gray eyes. He wondered how long he'd stood there staring at her.

When he climbed into bed that night, patiently awaiting another vivid dream, Thomas wondered how he could feel so bad for a girl he knew nothing about.

After all, he didn't even know her name.

Chapter 2

*S*top *thinking about it.*

Warrenna saw it in her mind: wedged just beneath her heart was a hard sphere, like a marble. It throbbed with every heartbeat, swirling black and orange.

She imagined her blood flowing through the marble, every drop emerging a shade darker, a trace more contaminated.

Stop it. That doesn't help the craving. You know that.

Still, she couldn't help but wonder if the marble had been there on that playground in Denver when that wonderful smell had brought her lips to the gash in Scottie Templeton's leg.

She remembered the stunned faces of the other children, how they quickly turned to ridicule. Their singsong chants echoed in her mind: "*Ren*-na's a *blood*-sucker! *Ren*-na's a *blood*-sucker!"

Gee, Mom. Thanks for sparing me that humiliation ten years ago. Oh, that's right, you didn't! Instead you just lied to me. "There's no such thing as vampires, Renna. You're just different."

Warrenna rolled over, further entangling herself in her ball of blankets. Her gaze fell upon the pale blue light leaking around the curtains across the room. Morning had finally arrived.

"Warrenna," her father's voice came from the doorway. "It's time to get up, hon."

She rubbed her eyes. If she wasn't going to sleep in her bed, maybe she could do so at school. The drive out of the canyon was hypnotic enough. Then she'd just have to find a desk in the corner.

"Come on. You have to go."

She sighed. "Fine."

The shower cleared away some of the stickiness in her eyes, and her pale skin sucked up the moisture like a sponge. But she knew it would just matter of time before the skin on her elbows flaked and peeled like a snake shedding its scales.

When she finished bathing, Warrenna brushed her short, thick, reddish-brown hair. She combed it partway down her face so that some of the auburn locks hung peek-a-boo style in front of her right eye.

"All right, Renna," she told the tired gray eye in her reflection. "Let's survive another crappy day."

She pulled on a pair of men's dress slacks, slipped her bony arms into a long-sleeved violet shirt, and then eyed her figure in the mirror. She wondered if the loose material made her small breasts look even smaller.

She rolled her eyes. *Why should I care?*

Her father waited in the kitchen, idly buffing his fingernails against his black silk shirt as he leaned against a counter. "Eat quickly or you'll be late."

Warrenna yawned. "I'm not hungry."

"Try anyway."

She sighed again and started on a banana. The fruit was fresh, but tasted bland and flavorless. She choked down a swallow. "Where's Mom?"

"Sleeping." Richard wiped his black goatee with a napkin. "I'm taking you this morning."

Warrenna nodded. Dad wasn't a talker. Maybe she could get some sleep in the car.

The drive north from Tebon Canyon to Chiricahua High School took forty minutes, half of which was spent climbing the twisting road partway up, then all the way down Burnham Peak. Both of Warrenna's parents drove slowly and carefully, and her eyes glazed over each time they went down the mountain. She imagined the Volvo's smooth ride and soft leather seats had a great deal to do with her drowsiness.

Her eyelids were drooping shut when her father spoke. "Have you made any friends yet?"

"Oh, yeah, sure," Warrenna muttered. "I'm the most popular girl in school."

"Are you trying?"

She shook her head. "These kids have known each other all their lives. I don't think any of them are eager to hang out with the weird new girl. And if you ask me, the fewer people I have to lie to, the better."

"Your mother and I aren't asking you to lie. We're asking you to keep others out of our personal business. You know they could never understand our struggle."

"Whatever, Dad."

She stared out of the dark-tinted window. *We shouldn't be talking about this, because I shouldn't be here. I should be back in Bellingham with my friends.*

They reached the bottom of Burnham Peak and turned north onto Highway 20. The tall pines and Douglas firs gave way to scrubby mesquite, spindly yucca and endless barbed wire. Mountains filled each horizon, some nearby, some in the distance, but all brownish and baked. The morning sun shone brightly on the high desert, giving each cactus its own long shadow.

"I don't see why I'm still going to school," Warrenna muttered. "It's pretty pointless, considering what we are."

"I've explained this before, Renna," Richard replied. "If we are to find infected people, we have to be part of society. We'll never help anyone if we live like hermits. It's why I have my night job, and why you're going to high school like a regular kid. You have to get used to being around humans."

Warrenna cringed at the word *humans*.

Like I needed another reminder of how different I am.

"How are you feeling?"

"How do you think?" Warrenna snapped. Normally conversations with her father lasted two minutes at most. She definitely preferred his old silence.

"Listen, Renna. I'm sorry we had to move when we did. I know it's been hard for you."

"I'd finally made some friends, Dad," Warrenna said sadly. "I liked Bellingham. There was green grass, for one thing. And we had rain, and the ocean, and Seattle was just down the road. Look at us." She waved at the yellow fields of deer grass dotted with brown clumps of mesquite: "We're in the middle of the desert here."

"I know it's been hard," Richard repeated, "but we're not going back. It isn't safe. Bascomville may be small and isolated, but we're safe here, and that's the most important thing."

Warrenna bowed her head. "I know."

If only Mom had avoided that car accident. I'd still be cursed, but at least I'd be home.

They reached the stucco façade of Chiricahua High School, and Richard pulled up as close as he could to the main entrance.

Warrenna opened the door. "Who's going to pick me up?"

"I will."

"Is Mom all right?"

"She will be. Have a good day. Make some friends."

"Yes, sir," she muttered, and started her quick walk to the entrance.

As she strode down the bright concrete path, Warrenna felt the familiar pressure of sunlight on her skin, like a dull butter knife scraping every exposed inch. But she was more concerned about the heat. It was barely March, and yet she didn't need a jacket. What would July be like?

Then she noticed the denim jackets and satin windbreakers on the students slowly shuffling by. And then she remembered.

I don't feel the cold like these kids do.

She folded her arms and held them close to her sides so she would look as cold as the next girl.

Before she reached the building's shadow, a man in a white suit stopped her and asked for the time. She smirked, then pointed at the giant clock above the four sets of double glass doors.

"Of course." he said, then tipped his white fedora and walked toward the parking lot.

Warrenna shook her head. *Guess some people are just dense.*

The relief of shade faded quickly as the prospect of another boring, lonely day of school emerged in Warrenna's thoughts. She wandered down the wide hallway toward her locker and tried to look at the bright side: in her second-hour art class, she could work on her paintings all period. Maybe Ms. Coleman would let her work in the art room during lunch again.

Suddenly her breath caught in her throat. A bitter, mouth-watering scent filled her nostrils. Human blood.

Warrenna's stomach rumbled and her vision sharpened. A quick look revealed a boy holding a fistful of dripping tissue to his nose as he leaned against a wall.

The black marble inside her pulsed. Her sides quivered. The tips of her fingers burned and the gums around her eyeeteeth tingled in anticipation.

She took a deep breath and bent over, pretending to tie up her boots as she fought off the excitement.

"Come on, Renna," she whispered. "Fight it. Like Mom and Dad say, 'You'll live with them all your life. You can't let the craving consume you.'"

Warrenna closed her eyes, but the black marble appeared in the darkness. Orange swirled in her vision, like lava flowing down a black mountain.

Release me.

Her own voice growled inside her.

Let me show us what we are capable of. You will see. There is no sound more pleasing than a scream of fear. No taste that comes close to young, living blood. It is joy, it is rapture!

No. She forced herself to take a couple of steps, fighting the voice. *If I set you free, I'll die. And so will my parents, and everyone else who fights the curse.*

Eager to think about something else, Warrenna looked around as she moved away from the compelling aroma. Students crowded the hall, most chatting and laughing in groups.

A girl in a cheerleader outfit walked near her, happily chatting with another girl about which boy she hoped would ask her to the prom. Her eyes were bright, her hair vibrant and bouncy. Nothing like Warrenna's would ever be.

"Clueless," Warrenna whispered. "Here you are walking five feet from a vampire, and you're worried about some stupid dance."

But Warrenna knew she had that same conversation, once upon a time. Only it was about homecoming, and about Corbett.

The memories had a fuzzy feeling, like she was trying to remember a dream from a lifetime ago. She shook her head, and more than ever wanted to be back in Bellingham. *I also don't want to be cursed. I guess what I want doesn't really matter, does it?*

"Hey."

A boy from third-hour English stood before her. His short brown hair didn't want to stay in place, and his eyes were blue as the pale desert sky.

He smiled, which immediately brought Warrenna's guard up. "Hi," he said. "I just wanted to apologize for yesterday."

"Apologize? For what?"

"For staring. During third hour. I didn't mean anything by it."

"You were staring at me?"

"Um, yeah. Remember when I passed around the handout? When I stopped at your desk I felt kinda weird and just sorta spaced out." He trailed off, and his bright eyes fixed on her shoulder.

Warrenna wondered why he wouldn't look at her face. But then she felt something spark in the left side of her chest, just beneath her heart.

It was that imaginary marble again. But it wasn't black anymore. In her mind, it was blue, like the boy's eyes.

And it was warm.

Relief swept over her, like a cool ocean breeze on a hot, muggy day. The feeling reminded her of her childhood, of wandering around groves of oak trees in a neighborhood far away from this lonely desert. She remembered how safe she felt when she saw the pallid headstones of the Benzel Street Cemetery. That meant home was just around the corner.

She blinked. The boy was looking at her. "Um, what?" she said.

"I mean it. I really am bad with names." He gave her a weak smile. "Ask any of my friends. You know, in one ear, out the other."

"Oh. It's Renna."

He cocked his head. "Is that short for something?"

"Yeah. For Warrenna."

He squinted, so she added, "Like Warren, with a 'nuh' at the end. War-ren-nuh."

"Oh." He grinned. "That's an interesting name you have there."

"I didn't pick it."

"No, I guess you didn't." His smile vanished.

"What name did your parents pick for you?"

"Oh." His eyes were shiny with sudden tears, and he looked away. "Thomas. My friends call me Tom."

"Are you okay, Thomas?"

"Yeah." His voice was rough now, and he sniffed. "I just think I'm having that feeling again, and it's a little freaky, and, uh, I gotta go."

Thomas hurried away with his head down and his hand covering his eyes.

"Nice to meet you, Thomas."

She wondered if he was crying, and if she had done something to provoke his tears. She shrugged. *What do I care?*

At least the marble was cold and black again.

Chapter 3

Even as she held him in the soothing waters of Telikiva Stream, his eyes smoldered like a nighttime forest fire glowing on the mountainside.

She held his back as the water washed over him. His teeth were set in a grimace of pain, the same one he wore every day and every night of his journey.

With one hand, she gently peeled the bandage from his thigh. The cool water flowed into the blackened wound, but his expression never changed.

"Does it hurt?"

His angry eyes stared at the sky. "It always hurts. It will hurt until it kills me."

She said nothing. The thin white trees, barren of leaves, reached to the sky like skeletal fingers.

Suddenly his hand clutched her arm. His eyes were wide, and his grimace was gone.

"Mother-to-Doves," he gasped. "Have you ever heard the Sky-God?"

She nodded. "I have heard the Sky-God in the rumbles of the summer storms, and in the silence of the winter snowfall."

"But has She ever spoken to you?"

Mother-to-Doves shook her head, her long braid swaying back and forth.

"She just spoke to me," he said. The fire in his eyes was gone, quenched to smoke. "Her voice is soothing, like the rain among the trees. I have heard it before, but I did not know it till now."

"What did She say?"

He looked back to the sky. "She told me that it was all right to be afraid. She said my fear does not make me a coward."

He pulled himself to his feet, and stood beside her in the stream. Tears spilled out of his eyes. "I'm afraid, Mother-to-Doves," he said. "I'm afraid I won't complete my journey. I won't return to the land."

She smiled. "You have no reason to be afraid, Eyes-of-Dawn-Sky." She placed his headdress back onto his head. The red feather rose high above his black hair. "For I will be with you until the end."

Warrenna gasped, and the stream disappeared. Back were the chalkboards, inspirational posters, and chattering students of third-hour English.

She rubbed her eyes. She could still feel the man's touch on her arm, and her auburn hair felt heavy, like it was wet.

She looked around. No one had reacted to her gasp.

Before the details escaped her, she quickly sketched the lines of the water, the leafless aspen, and the man with the feather in his hair.

The severe angles of the man's face and the colorless trees

had the makings of an interesting pen-and-ink project. The red feather would really stand out against such a stark background.

She looked across the room to Thomas. He didn't notice her catnap, either. He wore a big smile as he passed notes with the pretty blonde girl in front of him.

Warrenna was glad he was happy again, but didn't know why. Maybe the sleepiness had her addled.

She yawned and began folding sheets of notebook paper precisely to form tiny, hardened shapes. Her goal was to make a crane in less than five minutes. She tried to fold quietly as she squinted at the clock. *How long is it till lunch?*

"Naw, Sunnyslope has the big dude in the middle. We're playing St. Francis. They don't have a center."

"No, St. Francis has the big guy. Name's Overgaard, some Swedish dude that always goes to his left. You're thinking of Xavier's all-guard lineup."

"You're both wrong. Xavier has the blond cheerleader with the rack, San Felipe has the big dude, and St. Francis plays full-court press all game."

Thomas glanced up from his hamburger to find most of the Coyotes basketball team looking at him.

"So who's right, Gelbaugh?"

Thomas spoke up so the whole table could hear him over the din of the cafeteria. "Okay, here's the deal. Overgaard, who's actually a Dane, plays for San Felipe. He's left-handed, doesn't like to face the basket, and torched us for twenty-six in our own gym. Mingus has the all-guard lineup that can shoot threes but can't rebound worth a crap, and Xavier plays full-court press all game 'cuz they got no half-court offense. This Saturday, we're playing Sunnyslope, who's got the coach that cusses every *goddamn* sentence and the cheerleader with the rack and pigtails that renders Rodriguez here useless at the free-throw line 'cuz he likes his girls *young*."

Everyone laughed, even Corwyn, who threw some French fries that Thomas easily ducked. "'Course," Thomas added, "I only know all this 'cuz I got lotsa time to watch stuff while I'm ridin' pine."

"But you're right," Brendan said with a big smile. "You're always right. We're gonna have to get C-Rod some blinders for when he goes to the line."

Corwyn gave Brendan the finger, then said, "Dude, can I help it if she's bustin' out?"

Brendan shrugged. "S'part of the game. Like the crowd, or the mascot yelling your name. You gotta focus. And if we focus on defense, we'll blow these jokers out of the gym."

"Aww, *yeah!*" everyone said at once.

Thomas smiled. He liked their chances against Sunnyslope. They had no answer for Brendan, and the more one-sided the game became, the more playing-time he'd get.

But then his heart sank. *Great, I'll get ten stupid minutes in another irrelevant game.*

His eyes widened. *Whoa. Where did* that *come from?*

Tears burned his eyes, and his throat tightened up. The feelings reminded him of that morning, when he apologized to the new girl.

He looked around. Sure enough, Warrenna stood in the hallway outside the cafeteria. She shuffled toward the soda machines with her chin resting on her chest. Her black shoulder bag pulled down the entire left side of her thin body. She never looked toward him.

Thomas clenched his teeth. Why was she messing with him like this? What did he ever do to her?

But then he shook his head. *Why am I so sure she's responsible?*

"Hey, Tom."

It didn't make any sense. Why should he care anything about her?

"I thought you already had a girl."

Thomas blinked. Brendan raised his dark eyebrows. "Remember Mariah? Cute blond chick? You've been puttin' mad moves on her in English for the last month. What's the matter, no longer interested?"

"You mind if I give her a shot?" Corwyn added.

"Up yours," Thomas muttered. "Look, Mariah's the one I'm chasing, okay? That Renna chick just rubs me the wrong way."

"That *who* chick?"

"Never mind." He stood and shoved his tray to Corwyn. "Take my tray, will ya? I gotta take a leak."

"Whatever, man."

Thomas bowed his head and trudged out of the cafeteria. Warrenna's gloomy gray eyes floated in his vision, and his stomach churned like he'd eaten some bad Mexican food.

Something's going on here. I have to talk to Renna again, find out who she is. Maybe I've met her before and just can't remember.

Just then, a patch of blue flashed in the corner of his eye. He took another couple of steps, then stopped.

A painting hung on the wall, just above eye-level. It depicted a man riding a horse in front of gray tree trunks that blocked out the sky. The rider wore a deep blue cloak, and the horse's coat was sleek and black, like a raven. A triangle of white fur gleamed between the horse's shiny eyes.

Thomas's eyes tingled like a sleeping limb. "Ufer," he whispered. "His steed."

The rider was leaning forward in his saddle, and though the face was small, Thomas could make out a grim, clenched expression.

It's Yannic. He's hurt.

Thomas's eyes rolled up into half-closed lids. He had dreamt of that man. He had *been* that man.

A name sprang to his lips: "Natalie."

He remembered now: Yannic and Natalie grew up in the same village, and were friends throughout their childhood. But when she married into nobility, Yannic didn't see her for many years.

Then, on the night of the painting, a group of bandits attacked Natalie's new family as they traveled through this thick forest. Yannic appeared out of nowhere to fend them off.

Natalie rode out to speak to him. She wanted to thank him, Thomas supposed. He remembered trying his hardest to ignore the terrible pain in his side as Natalie approached with her torch held high in her right hand.

Bong, bong.

The world twisted with each clang of the end-of-lunch bell, and Thomas slumped forward into the smooth concrete wall. As the room slowed its spin, he found a placard before his eyes:

The Wounded Rider, by Warrenna Dennison
Second-Hour Painting II.

Thomas shook his aching head. This girl had some serious explaining to do.

Flip.

"How much would you expect to pay for the Ronco Juicer-Sluice? Fifty dollars? One hundred dollars? Thanks to this special offer, if you call in the next fifteen minutes..."

Flip.

"Another fifteen dead in Gaza as Israeli-Palestine clashes continue..."

Flip.

"'Least I don't go round BLEEP BLEEP for ten bucks a shot!" the woman's voice shouted.

"OOOOOHHH! You hussy!"

It was past one in the morning, and Warrenna was nowhere near sleep. But that was okay. She liked this particular talk show. *Ruby Frohm* was on every night, and sure, Warrenna had her problems, but at least she wasn't like Crystal, an overweight nineteen-year-old mother of two who wore too much eye makeup.

Warrenna's stomach turned when she realized that Crystal didn't have it that bad. "At least you chose to make your life the way it is," she told the image on the television. "At least you weren't born with a curse."

She shuddered and rolled over. Now the screen on her twelve-inch TV was upside-down.

Flip.

There was a soft rap on her door. "Come in," she said without moving.

Alexandria took a step inside, swaying as she moved. She leaned heavily on a polished black cane that Warrenna hadn't seen before.

"I see you aren't sleeping," Alexandria said. "Your father tells me you haven't eaten. Is the craving bothering you?"

"No," Warrenna mumbled. "I just haven't felt like eating."

Alexandria took a few unsteady steps toward Warrenna's wooden easel, shifting her velvety blue bathrobe to ease herself down upon a stool. Her reddish-brown hair hung unevenly and black in places, like it had been singed in a fire.

Warrenna raised her head from the bed. "What about you, Mom? Are you all right?"

"I'll be fine." Alexandria's voice was hoarse, like she'd been shouting, or crying. "I had a little setback, and my last cleansing was a bit demanding. I'm more worried about you."

Warrenna rolled her eyes.

"I know this has been difficult," Alexandria continued. "I wish we didn't have to move when we did. The young people here are probably…Well. It must be difficult to get along."

Warrenna didn't say anything as she flipped channels. She didn't feel like having this conversation again.

"Look at it this way. You just need to go for a few more months. Then it will be over."

Warrenna sat up, but kept her eyes on the television. "Yeah, and then what?"

"Well, if you would like to go to college," Alexandria said, brightening, "Southern Arizona is in Maldecido. Not far away at all. Your father and I lived there for some time when we were younger, and we still have friends in the area. We can make some arrangements. You would be safe there."

"What if I don't want to go to SAU?"

"Then the local community college here in Bascomville has many programs that you might be interested in."

Warrenna sighed. "Why do I bother?"

"What, hon?"

"I said, why do I bother? Why do I bother going to school? Why do I even bother to breathe? What I want makes no difference at all in what I do. I may as well be a zombie!"

"Calm down, Warrenna," Alexandria said, her voice firm. "You are far too important for us to make any decision without your safety being the most important factor in the process."

"Yeah, I'm *so* important. So important that I don't get to live my own life."

Alexandria's dark eyes narrowed. "Warrenna, look at me. You are going to do great things, things that will affect thousands of lives. You may not want your role now, but when you're older, you'll see."

"What *things*, Mother?" Warrenna spat. "What exactly am I going to do? You don't even know. You just *think* I'm this important because Zera tells you."

"And she would tell you too, if you prayed to her."

Warrenna looked away. *Here we go again.*

"You have to trust Zera," Alexandria continued. "Without her, you wouldn't be alive, and your father and I would have given in to our evil desires many years ago."

Warrenna closed her eyes and clenched her fists until they shook. "I know, Mother," she whispered. "I know very well that Zera is the only reason I'm here. That's exactly why I hate her so much."

Alexandria sighed deeply and rubbed her bony hands together. "Ah, Renna. I know you have trouble believing me. I also resented my existence when I was your age. I didn't choose to become a vampire. Neither did your father. We took our safe, ordinary lives for granted, assuming we could take advantage of the opportunities our parents had provided for us. But when all that was changed, we didn't give up hope. We *fought*. We didn't stop pursuing our own happiness. We just had to acknowledge that happiness might not come in a form we anticipated."

Leaning heavily on the cane, Alexandria pushed herself to her feet and placed a hand on her daughter's shoulder. "Perspective is difficult to acquire at your age. Zera can help you obtain it, but you must want her help. And prayer is the best way to show your desire to our Goddess."

Warrenna stared at her knees as her mother turned to the door. "Try to get some sleep," Alexandria said. "You'll feel better."

Warrenna nodded, and her mother shuffled out of her room.

"Yeah, you and Dad didn't have any choice back then," she mumbled. "You had no one to blame but fate. But you had a choice sixteen years ago. You and your precious Zera chose to make me the way I am. You *chose* to put the beast inside me."

She rubbed her eyes. The tears were gone, replaced by sticky fatigue. "So this time around, I have someone to blame." A bitter chuckle escaped her. "Actually, it's more like a list of someones."

She turned upside-down again and watched to see if Crystal would take back her two-timing boyfriend.

Chapter 4

Thomas breathed deep as the warm water pounded his back. His memories of the last night's dream seemed to be swirling down the drain, and his thoughts moved inevitably to Warrenna's painting and his strange reaction to it. The new perspective inspired some changes in the short story, and Mrs. Hayes was right. With the added context, all of Yannic's actions carried more meaning. The story was much more interesting.

He wondered how Warrenna's painting could have done this to him. Could she have had the same dream? Was that even possible?

Thomas pictured Yannic turning to ride away. And then the typed passage appeared in his hand.

Suddenly the water stopped, and his ears filled with the sound of teenagers walking and talking.

"Um, can I get to my locker please?"

A mousy-haired girl looked up to him over her thick glasses. His left hand held the short story and his right held his backpack at his shoulder. And he had no idea how he came to be standing in that hallway in Chiricahua High School.

No memories came. There was nothing about stepping out of the shower, eating breakfast or driving down Carter Avenue. He didn't know if his car started up on the first try, or if he had to try two or three times.

"Um, do you mind?" the mousy girl said.

He mumbled an apology and stepped out of her way.

Thomas's eyes dashed back and forth as he tried to figure out what had just happened. Maybe his mind drifted away while he stood in the shower, and his body went on autopilot, keeping to the pattern he'd followed for the last six months. *Like during finals, when I went two days without sleep. I was like a robot going from class to class.*

The smell of black pepper tickled his nose, so he must have eaten some eggs for breakfast.

"Warrenna."

The name came out of him before he formed it in his mind. He was standing in the same hallway where he talked to her yesterday.

"I would have woken up if I saw her," he whispered. "I would've. I *would have!*"

The bell rang, and Thomas's heart sank. Class was starting. He had to wait until tomorrow to get any answers from Warrenna.

But maybe she was late. Maybe he didn't wake up when she walked right by, or something else he hadn't thought of. He could see her in third hour.

Or maybe he could see her before then.

Warrenna drifted down the wide common hallway, gulping the Mountain Dew as fast as she could. *Sure, get sleepy now, just in time for the only class I want to be awake in.*

The visual arts classrooms were just around the corner, but as she turned, she collided with a man in a white suit.

"Whoops!" the man said, and smiled at her with impossibly white teeth. "Terribly sorry about that."

Warrenna didn't even drop her soda, but she got a static-electricity shock from touching the man's jacket.

When she looked up, she recognized him. It was the old man who asked her for the time in the parking lot yesterday. He wore a short white beard and had small blue eyes. Warrenna wondered why someone would wear the same suit two days in a row.

"Hey Renna!"

Warrenna looked past the man to see Thomas's lean frame jogging up the hallway. He waved a manila folder like a castaway flagging down a cruise ship.

When he reached her, Warrenna started down the hall again. "Hello, Thomas. How are you?"

"Um, strange. I always feel strange around you. It's like you do it on purpose."

"Like I do what?"

"Nothing, forget it. Hey, has Mrs. Hayes ever given you anything of mine?"

She slowed her pace. "Has who ever given me what?"

"Mrs. Hayes, our English teacher." Thomas rubbed his tan forearm. "Has she ever given you anything that I've written?"

"Uh, no. Why do you ask?"

"Your painting. The one in the hallway, *Wounded Rider.* Where did you get the idea for it?"

She shrugged. "I don't know. Some movie or something."

Thomas's face fell, and Warrenna took the initiative: "You wanted me to say something else, didn't you?"

They stopped beside the entrance to Ms. Coleman's room. Thomas's bright eyes darted back and forth. Save for the man in the white suit leaning against a wall at least a hundred feet away, the hall was empty.

"Look," Thomas whispered, "I need you to do me a favor."

"Oh, yeah?"

He held up the folder. "I need you to read this story, and give it back to me third hour. Please, I really need you to do this for me."

Warrenna widened her eyes in mock wonder. "Gosh, read a whole story in one hour? Gee, I don't know."

Thomas winced, and Warrenna studied his face. His jaw was clenched, and his eyes were serious. "Fine," she said, and snatched the folder from his hand. "If it's *that* important to you, I'll read your little story."

"Good. I appreciate it. Thank you." Tears welled up in his eyes. Frustrated and suddenly embarrassed, he said, "Uh, thank you. I'll see you next hour." Then he turned and jogged away.

Warrenna shook her head. *Where does he get off, demanding answers and asking for a favor?*

He did look worried, though. He didn't smile, even once. And this was the second time he was on the verge of tears around her.

Why should I care? I don't know this guy. And he definitely doesn't know me.

But still, she didn't want anyone upset. If reading his little story would make him happy, she had the time.

Thomas tapped his foot against his desk as he made mincemeat of the inside of his cheek. What if his strange dreams had some kind of purpose behind them after all? What if Warrenna walked in looking amazed and teary-eyed, with a tale in her head from Natalie's perspective that his story brought out?

But what if the story *didn't* affect her? What if the similarities were just a coincidence? What if what happened to him when he saw her painting was actually a symptom of some mental illness?

Maybe there's something really wrong with me. Maybe my dreams are hallucinations. Maybe this morning was a blackout. Who knows what else is happening in my head?

Something waved in front of Thomas's face. He turned, wild-eyed, and Brendan quickly pulled his hand back.

"Hey, sorry. Didn't mean to scare you." Brendan peered into Thomas's eyes. "Are you all right, man? I mean, you sleepwalk through yesterday's practice and don't even blink when coach yells at you for daydreaming. Then you walk right by me and C-Rod this morning like we're not there. What's going on?"

"Uh, nothing." But then Warrenna appeared in the door. "Well, it's something I'm gonna take care of right now."

He hurried across the room, arriving at Warrenna's corner desk just as she fell into it. "So what do you think?" he asked.

She yawned. "It's really good. You know what you're doing with words."

He gave a frustrated sigh and stuck his hands in his back pocket. "I didn't want an opinion on my skill. I want to know if the story *meant* anything to you."

"What do you mean, 'meant?' What do you care what I think?"

Thomas chomped on the inside of his cheek and bowed his head. He couldn't come up with any way around telling her everything. He made sure no one was close enough to hear, and then began.

"Okay, here it is. That story came from a dream I had a while back, and when I looked at your painting yesterday, I swear the dream was happening again, I was *inside* it. Only I knew more about what was going on, 'cause I had another perspective."

Thomas could feel his throat tightening up again. His words were sounding strange enough. How crazy would he sound if he started telling Yannic and Natalie's story?

"Hey, Tommy boy."

He looked up to find Mariah's bright blue eyes staring back at him. He swallowed hard and held her gaze. "I'm kind of in the middle of something right now. I'll just be a minute."

Mariah's jaw dropped, but she recovered quickly. "Sure. Take your time."

Thomas looked back to Warrenna's dull gray eyes. She was staring at him, too.

That was when he felt the tears running down his cheeks.

"Damn." He wiped his face with the back of his hand. "Sorry."

"That's all right." She rubbed her shirttail between her fingers. "Do you have a car, Thomas?"

"What? Oh, yeah. Why?"

"I'd like to talk some more about this. Someplace," she moved her eyes from side to side, "more private. How about after school today? You'd have to take me home."

"Okay. Sure, that'd be good." He sniffed. "Listen, I'm sorry, I don't know what came over me."

"Hang on." She gestured to the tiny cell phone that was suddenly at her ear. "Hey, it's me. No, nothing's wrong. Listen, you don't have to come pick me up this afternoon. Because a friend of mine is giving me a ride, that's why. Unless I'm suddenly not allowed to have friends. Yeah. Okay. No, it'll be okay. Okay. Bye."

The bell rang, and she looked back at Thomas. "All right. Meet me at the main exit after sixth hour. We'll go somewhere and chat."

"Okay. Thanks." He turned to go.

"Tom? Your story?"

He whirled back around and took the pages from her. "Oh, yeah, thanks."

Thomas didn't look at any of his friends as he sat down at his desk.

"What was all that?" Mariah asked, loud enough for everyone nearby to hear.

"Oh, nothing." Thomas forced himself to smile through the plummeting feeling in his stomach. "She did this painting, and it reminded me of that scene in *Braveheart* when that girl gets her throat slit. We were talking about it, and I remembered the movie, and just kinda got overwhelmed by it."

Brendan stared at him, his eyes full of doubt.

"I know. She's a great artist, isn't she?" Thomas said, straining his voice to sound enthusiastic.

Brendan squinted at him, opened his mouth, then looked at Mariah. "Yeah," he finally said. "That's, um, a tough scene to forget. You see the love of someone's life killed right before your eyes."

Thomas sighed inwardly in relief. He knew Brendan didn't buy his story, but his friend was playing along, at least with Mariah around.

But now he had to come up with a story Brendan *would* believe.

Warrenna pulled her sketchbook out of her locker and slammed the door shut. Fifth hour was history, and the teacher wasn't big on class participation. Maybe she could work on that sketch of the man lying in the stream among those white-barked trees.

"Hey, Red!"

The words were shouted down the hall, but Warrenna kept walking. She wondered what the man in the stream was looking at.

"Wait up, Red."

A pretty blond girl grabbed her arm. Her blue eyes were clear and intense, and her smile seemed a little too sweet to use on someone she didn't know.

"My name's not Red," Warrenna told her.

"Yeah, I figured it probably wasn't." The girl let go of Warrenna's arm and walked beside her. "But I don't know what your name is, 'cause the only person you seem to talk to is Tommy, and when that happens he bursts into tears. What's up with that, by the way?"

Warrenna squinted. "What are you talking about?" Then she recognized the girl. She sat in front of Thomas in third-hour English. Warrenna had seen the two of them passing notes all week. "Oh, that. I don't know what his deal is. Why don't you ask him?"

"I did. He has his story, but I'd like to hear yours."

Warrenna thought for a second. Thomas had told her about his dream as though it was a secret. *Well Thomas, if you lied to this girl, you're on your own.*

"He said one of my paintings really affected him. There seems to be a lot more on his mind, though."

The girl frowned. "That's for sure."

"Listen, what's your name?"

"Mariah."

"Mariah, I'm Warrenna. It's nice to meet you. If you're worried about me going after your man, you can relax. He's not my type. And I've seen the way he looks at you." She grinned. "You've got nothing to worry about."

Mariah blushed and bit her lower lip. "Yeah, well, I'm just worried about him. He acts like a goof, but there's a lot going on inside him, you know?"

Warrenna shrugged. "Couldn't say." She paused at a classroom door. "This is my stop."

"Oh. Well, thanks. What was your name again?"

"Just call me Renna."

"Thanks, Renna. I'll see you in class."

"Uh-huh."

She waited for Mariah to turn a corner, then resumed down the hall, toward her actual classroom.

Chapter 5

Warrenna pushed through the river of students flowing to the parking lot, wondering how long it would take to meet up with Thomas. As small as Bascomville was, the high school was still populated by hundreds of kids.

But it didn't take long to find him. His pogo-stick hopping by the front door made it pretty easy.

She frowned. *I hope I didn't get his hopes up too high.*

Nothing about his story stood out, but the tears streaming down his face stung her eyes as if she were the one crying. She figured she could at least give him a private conversation. That would probably make her feel more human, too.

"Hey," he said when she reached him. "Did anything come to mind?"

"I really need a cup of coffee. I'd rather not discuss your dream 'till I get some java in me. You know any place we can go?"

"Uh, sure. There's A.J.'s. It's got a cappuccino machine, Italian sodas, and a bunch of different kinds of coffee."

Warrenna gestured to the streams of teenagers passing by them through the doors. "We gonna have lots of company?"

"I don't think so. You'll see."

"Okay. You don't think Mariah will get upset with you hanging with another girl, do you?"

His eyebrows rose. "Well, what Mariah doesn't know won't hurt her." He laughed. "And if she *does* mind, then I'm in better shape with her than I thought."

They started into the dusty parking lot. The afternoon sun blazed a brilliant yellow in the pale sky, so Warrenna quickly fished a pair of wraparound sunglasses out of her bag.

Thomas grinned. "You look like an old lady with those things on."

Warrenna glared at him, but she was happy to see his smile. "My eyes are really light-sensitive. I can't *believe* how bright it is here."

"You'll get used to it. Everybody does."

The sun was behind them as they walked, so Warrenna pulled her collar up to cover her neck. No skin was exposed, but her back and shoulders itched from the heat.

Warrenna told herself to relax. The shade was soon to come.

They reached a small brownish car that looked like it hadn't been washed in years. With a sweep of his hand, Thomas said, "Warrenna, meet the Beatermobile."

"Nice to meet you, Beater." She stroked the roof as though she was petting a cat. "Is it a boy or a girl?"

"Boy. Stick-shift."

"Ah. Does he have A-C?"

"Uh-huh."

"Good. I can't *believe* how hot it is here, either."

Thomas started the car, and they queued up to exit the parking lot. "So, you haven't lived here long, right?"

"Just about two months."

"Where'd you move from?"

Warrenna sighed and adjusted the sunshade. "A little town near the coast in Washington State. We had trees, we had the ocean, and it actually rained. It never rains here, does it?"

"Actually, we have thunderstorms every day during the monsoons."

"That's what my mother said. I can't imagine it's worth the wait."

He shrugged. "They're pretty cool. The lightning over the mountains can be pretty awesome."

"I'll watch for it."

Thomas steered the car out of the parking lot and onto the road. "So, what brings you to my corner of Arizona?"

Warrenna winced, and nervously dug through her shoulder bag to retrieve an old flyer. "It's kind of a long, boring story."

Thomas grinned again. "Lucky for you, I happen to like long, boring stories. I write them all the time."

"Heh." She folded the flyer in two precise places. "Well, my parents grew up here, and my mother had to get, uh, transferred, so she picked a place she was already familiar with."

Thomas nodded and gestured at her hands. "What are you doing there?"

"Oh, nothing. Just a little origami. Keeps my fingers nimble for painting."

He watched her with genuine interest. "Cool. What are you making?"

"A heart. See?" Warrenna held up the paper, but then she felt silly. "Here, you can have it." She slipped the heart into his glove compartment.

He smiled. "I'll let Beater keep it."

They stopped at the Highway 20 intersection and watched the cars and pickups race by on the wide, dusty blacktop.

"Hey, Thomas," Warrenna said, and he looked at her. "It's been, like, five minutes, and you're not crying."

He blushed and rolled his eyes. "Yeah, I'm sorry about that. I don't know what came over me."

"I'm just teasing you." She smiled. It felt good to tease someone again.

Thomas turned the car into a strip mall parking lot and eased the Escort beneath a sheltered overhang.

"Thanks for the shade," Warrenna said. "Guess I don't have Arizona eyes just yet."

"No problem. A.J.'s is over there, between the Cheap Cigs and Sammy's Salon."

Warrenna immediately liked the feel of A.J.'s Cafe as soon as she walked in because it was dim enough to remove her shades. Soft jazz played from speakers high on the walls, which reminded her of the Blue Tulip in Bellingham. She and Melissa had spent many an hour at that little coffeehouse sipping coffee and talking about boys. Any place that reminded her of the "BluTu" couldn't be all bad.

They sat at one of the tiny tables across from the bar, a dark cherry piece with polished brass knobs. "This is really nice," Warrenna said.

"Yeah. My mom works in the complex by the hospital around the way. She likes a quiet place to have lunch. Business doesn't pick up here 'til pretty late."

The waitress, a woman in her forties with black hair and a soft French accent, took their drink orders: a banana smoothie for Thomas, a double espresso for Warrenna.

Warrenna waited for her to leave, then asked, "So, what do kids do for fun around here? Tell me this isn't the sort of town where y'all go cow-tippin' every Friday night."

"No, no. Wednesdays are *much* better for tippin'. Not as many deputies out."

"Tell me you're messing with me."

Thomas tipped back an imaginary cowboy hat, and mimed

spitting into a spittoon. "Why, yes'm," he replied in a John Wayne drawl, "I reckon I am at that." He snorted and laughed. "We're not exactly a cow-town out here. Bascomville is like any other town, I guess. We've got our little theater, and our little park, and our little mall. And Maldecido's a pretty cool place. It's a college town about an hour north. There's always events going on at SAU. Lotta good concerts. I've been to Lomax Auditorium at least a dozen times."

"Oh, yeah?" Warrenna imagined twangy singers with enormous hairdos and/or belt buckles. But she asked anyway. "Who was the last act you saw?"

Thomas rubbed his neck. The blender whirred behind the bar. "Ever hear of Ancestor Cult?"

Warrenna's jaw dropped. "Are you serious?"

Thomas blushed. "Yeah, I know their fans are kind of creepy. But they do this one song. It's this amazing voice singing in Latin along with a violin. Whenever I hear it, I get hypnotized. I think I heard it in a dream once, or in a song like it anyway. It really stuck with me."

"That's *The Mirror Cannot Lie*. Great song."

His eyes lit up. "You've heard it?"

She nodded. "I saw the Cult in Seattle last year. I had to sneak out of the house, which made my parents furious. But the show was worth the four weeks I was grounded."

Thomas grinned. "Huh... I had to go by myself. My friends still give me crap about being a closet goth. I mean, great music is great music, and just because most of their fans have more piercings than fingers doesn't make the Cult's music any less amazing."

"Wait. You went by yourself?"

He shrugged again. "No one would go with me."

"That's funny, I went alone too. None of my friends wanted to go either. But I just had to hear that line in *Floating Upstream*. It's my favorite line ever written."

"Which line is that?"

Warrenna bit her lower lip and looked up to one of the slowly rotating ceiling fans. "It's the one that goes: 'No one, no one can stop what is coming.' The music stopped when she reached that line, and the crowd went absolutely silent."

"And you felt like she was singing to you alone," Thomas finished. He closed his eyes and smiled. "The rest of the crowd was gone, and it was just you. You and that breathtaking voice."

Thomas held the pose for a moment, lost in his reverie. Warrenna pictured him standing in a darkened concert hall, surrounded by strangers, his eyes closed, reveling in the music without a care for what happened around him.

Then Warrenna imagined herself standing on the opposite end of the same hall at that same moment, her eyes open but not seeing Thomas. Then, by chance, she would happen to turn his way. And then he would feel her eyes on him and look, and they would smile, for they knew that this moment, this music, this wordless connection from across an auditorium was the only thing that really mattered. Image, cliques, the condition you were born with, all that was meaningless. He would feel it all, and would move to her, his steps in time with the beat, and he would hold out his hand….

"Do you believe in fate, Renna?"

She blinked. "Fate?"

"'No one can stop what is coming,'" Thomas quoted. "Sounds like fate to me."

The waitress arrived and set their drinks on the table. When she left, Warrenna's eyes bore into Thomas's. "Yes, I believe in fate. I have to. I'd go crazy if I didn't. What about you?"

"I don't know. Fate is fun to talk about, but I think it's mostly the stuff of dreams." He took a long sip of his smoothie. "Speaking of dreams, do you mind if we talk about the story and the dream now?"

"Sure."

"Did you remember anything? Maybe a dream you had?"

Warrenna's eyes drifted to a watercolor sunset hanging on the wall. "Well, the situation sounds familiar. Like I've heard that kind of story before."

"Oh."

He sounded disappointed. She hurried on. "I mean, I guess it's possible. I get ideas for my paintings from all sorts of things, TV, movies, other paintings. My dreams are bound to influence my art."

"But you didn't have any great revelation."

"No."

Thomas's shoulders sagged.

"You shouldn't take coincidences so hard, Thomas. It's not good for you."

He shrugged and mumbled into his smoothie.

"Why does this matter so much?" Warrenna said. "You've obviously been pretty broken-up about it."

He started to speak, but then stopped and looked hard into her dull gray eyes. "Renna, can you keep a secret?"

Warrenna nodded, biting her lower lip to keep from saying, *you have no idea.*

Thomas took a deep breath and leaned forward. "Ever since I can remember, I've had really vivid dreams. Every single night I'm fully immersed, all senses. I've smelled the salt water of the greenest ocean, tasted the hottest red pepper, felt freezing ice or broiling sun on my skin. In one dream, I got stabbed in the leg, and I felt the pain, and the blood flowing down my knee."

He frowned. Warrenna froze. *I didn't just lick my lips when he mentioned blood, did I?* She quickly took a sip of her drink. "Go on."

He nodded. "I think I was eight when I realized that I dream different from anyone else. Well, anyone else I know about. I read about falling dreams or dreams where you can't move your legs, or your teeth fall out, or you go to school naked. Nothing weird like that ever happens in my dreams. But the thing is *I've* never been in them. Well, I guess it's me, but not with any face or body I recognize. And I've never seen anyone I know in these dreams. When I was twelve my mother suggested I start writing them down for the story ideas."

He shook his head. "Sorry, I'm rambling. Anyway, yesterday—there I was—standing in front of your painting, watching my dream play out again. Only it was from a different angle, and I learned some things about what was happening. My actions in the dream made more sense, but there's no reason why. Why your painting? Why you?"

He shrugged again, settled back into his chair and stared at the checkered floor. "Maybe I'm just crazy."

Warrenna leaned forward. "Sounds to me like you have a gift. You've got an endless supply of story material, for one thing. I've already seen one result, and it's really great."

"Yeah, I guess." He ran a hand through his hair. "Sometimes I think maybe the dreams are bad for me. Like maybe I'm not getting the subconscious release I need. Maybe that's why I flipped out yesterday."

Warrenna frowned. "I don't know how you'd be able to tell that. Frankly, I'm jealous. I never remember my dreams. I'd love to dream half as vivid as you say you do. I think dreams are important. They take your mind away. All your troubles vanish for a few hours every night. You don't have to worry about who you really are."

She stopped. *Who you really are.*

"Yeah, you're probably right. I know I take the dreams for granted. I just can't help but feel like a freak sometimes."

"I don't think you're a freak, Thomas. Maybe a little *freaky*," she grinned, "but not a freak. And I think Mariah probably agrees with me."

His face tightened. "She doesn't know about the dreaming. Nobody knows. Just you and my mom."

Warrenna put her hand over her heart. "Your secret is safe with me. Though *I* don't think you have anything to be ashamed of."

She blinked. *A secret to be ashamed of.*

"I appreciate it." The John Wayne drawl returned. "I reckon you're an all-right lady, Miss Warrenna, that I do."

He grinned and downed the rest of his drink, but then his eyes bulged when he saw a clock on the wall. "Wow, we'd better go. I've got homework to do, and we've got a decent drive in front of us." He pointed to her espresso. "About done?"

She frowned. "Yeah. Um, sure."

As they paid for the drinks, Warrenna's breath went short, like a hundred sobs had built up in her lungs and the slightest disappointment could make her explode. *What's going on with me all of a sudden?*

They returned to the car, and she absently answered Thomas's questions on what route to use to take her home. The ache in her heart steadily grew, but she couldn't figure out why. She just made a connection with someone for the first time in months, and he was a sweet guy. So why did she feel so bad?

Thomas turned the Beatermobile south on Highway 20 and accelerated. The sun still shined through Warrenna's window, so she arranged the tiny sunshade to keep the rays from stinging her pale face.

"If you don't mind," Thomas said over the hum of the engine, "I'd like to show you some more of my dreams. In the stories I've written, I mean. And maybe I could look at some more of your paintings to see if I weird out again."

"I don't know," she said, but wasn't sure Thomas heard her. "I don't know. I don't think that's a good idea."

He drummed his fingers on the steering wheel. "Look, I've got this weird thing about me, and I'm looking for anything to explain why I, of all people, dream this way every single night. If you had something weird about you, wouldn't you want to explore anything that might give you some clue as to why you are the way you are?"

Warrenna's breath stopped, like a pair of powerful hands had suddenly throttled her. "Maybe...maybe you just are what you are. Maybe there's no reason why. Like you said. No fate, no reason why. For anything."

She closed her eyes. Sure, it was fun to have coffee with a boy, to chat about music, dreams and fate. It was exciting, sparked some dreaming, and chased the loneliness away.

But this only happened because I forgot what I really am. And when I forget what I am, I put everyone around me in danger.

"Turn left up there," she said. "On Tebon Canyon Road."

Thomas dutifully turned the wheel, and they began the winding climb up Burnham Peak.

The black marble entered Warrenna's vision, but now, dark branches grew from its center, crawling up to wrap around her heart. *I should know better. It's not safe for me to dream. I'll just end up killing someone.*

She knew she could do what her parents asked: she could blend into Thomas's world of hope and endless possibilities. But now it was clear that she would never belong there. And that meant she was in for a lifetime of loneliness.

It was all Warrenna could do to keep from beating her fists on the Escort's dusty dashboard. She could scarcely believe that Thomas's eyes had once given her a sense of relief.

The Beatermobile slipped into the shadows of the pines. Warrenna looked at his eyes again. They looked ahead at the road, but they also bounced back and forth with thought as he tried to convince her to look at his dreams.

And then she knew what she had to do.

Ice water gushed from her heart down into her bowels, and

she clenched her fists so hard that her fingernails dug tiny holes into her palms. She *did* have a say in what happened to her. She had the ultimate word, the final decision.

The force of that resolution made her breath quiver. *Maybe I was relieved because I somehow knew that Thomas would get me to this point.*

"Renna?"

"You don't know how good you've got it."

"What?"

"Nothing. That's me right there." She pointed. "Don't go on the road."

"Uh, all right."

He brought the car to a stop next to a wide dirt road that branched off the pavement. Tall fir trees and high bushes stood on either side of the path, blocking out the late-afternoon sun. The path curved out of sight about twenty yards away. Warrenna opened her door.

"Look," Thomas said, "please think about it. I won't take up too much of your time. Five more dreams, five more paintings, and then I'll leave you alone. Promise."

She turned to him, her face clenched in anguish. "You need to stay away from me, Thomas. Forget you ever knew me. It's for your own good."

He blinked. "What are you talking about?"

"I'm bad news, Thomas." She bowed her head. "The more time you spend with me, the more danger you put yourself in." She climbed out of the car and closed the door.

Thomas reached across to roll down the passenger window. "Wait!" he yelled. "Renna! Why? What danger?"

Warrenna shouted her answer without stopping or turning around.

"The less you know, the safer you are!"

Chapter 6

The silence in the bathroom was thick, broken only by the occasional drip onto the calm surface of water. Warrenna felt her sides caving in, like she stood on the floor of a deep swimming pool.

She flicked on the overhead fan, and the hum relieved some of the pressure from the silence. She slipped out of her robe and hung it over the towel rack.

Then she dragged one of her easel-stools to the door and wedged the seat beneath the knob.

She tested the door; it didn't budge. Satisfied, she eased into the water.

Her limbs trembled with the anticipation of what she was about to do. *It's about to happen. Here, I take control of my life.*

She listened through the ceiling fan's whir for any sign of her father. He wasn't due to rouse her for two more hours.

No sound.

A clean razor sat on the soap dish. Warrenna slid the edge across a fingertip. Dark blood pooled into her fingernail, and she paused.

Her hands were shaking. She couldn't make them stop.

She took a deep breath. *I have to do this. There's no other way out.*

A drop of water formed at the spout as she stared at her bloody fingernail.

Maybe I'll start over. With a better chance. With cleaner blood.

The drop fell to the surface with a *plip*. The fan droned on.

Maybe I'll be a bird in my next life. Maybe I'll swim the skies and scratch the clouds.

She smiled, and her fingers were calm again. She found the spot on her wrist and closed her eyes.

Pain ripped through her forearm. She bit her lip to keep from crying out. But she knew that pain wouldn't tell her what she needed to know. She had to look.

It took a moment to gather the courage. She opened her eyes.

A gash ran from the end of her palm three inches down her wrist. Crimson blood welled up in the wound, spilling down her pale forearm in branching streams. The rivulets flowed down her elbow and into the water, diffusing into pink mist.

If she made another cut, the pain would go away. She picked another spot and clamped her eyes shut.

She slashed again. It wasn't as painful as the first.

But when she opened her eyes, she found the razor still buried in her wrist. Blood spurted from the companion wound, soaking her hand.

The blade slipped out of her fingers, out of the gash, and splashed into the water, slowly sinking to rest on her stomach.

With shallow breaths, she watched the blood flow out of her wrist. Her heart pounded, her jaw quivered, her eyes bulged, but the pain vanished. Life still flowed out of her cuts, reddening her arm and turning the bathwater pink. But it didn't hurt anymore.

The first twinge of self-doubt sprouted in her. *Am I really ready to go?*

She had no idea what death was going to feel like. And who would find her?

She pictured her mother and father weeping over her pale, naked body as her corpse floated in a black pool.

They'll be devastated. They may even give up the fight, start feeding on people.

Warrenna's eyes filled with tears at the thought of her parents' despair.

But then she heard a child's voice in sing-song chant:

"Ren-na's a blood-sucker...."

She gritted her teeth. *Maybe my parents should have thought of that before making me like this. They should have pictured me here before bringing me into a world where I can never belong.*

She smiled wanly and slid back in the tub, picturing the black marble floating uselessly inside her as it ran out of blood to contaminate.

Take that, curse.

Her arm dropped into the water with a small splash. Blood erupted from the cuts, red smoke billowing from a black fire in her veins. But after a few slow breaths, she rested in pleasant warmth. It could have been another lazy Sunday afternoon in Bellingham, just lounging in the tub as her father yelled at the football game. She could almost hear him. "C'mon, play some defense!"

A Sunday where she didn't have to be anywhere, but she'd make a trip to Gigi's CDs anyway, to see that cute clerk with the red goatee. Maybe she would finally take his advice and buy his band's CD. The guitars would be hypnotic and dreamy, but still somehow convey a message of love without sounding sappy.

Sappy. She liked that word. It was a good way to describe most of the schlock on the movie screens.

Pain streaked across Warrenna's sleepy fantasy like a lightning bolt across a stormy evening sky. She shook her head and told herself she was just tired. A good, long sleep would make up for the past couple of months. The ache in her arm would be gone soon enough.

Her eyelids drooped closed.

She heard the imaginary song, its subtle bass line, the singer's matter-of-fact declarations of love that sent her heart soaring higher than any overwrought romantic poem ever had.

I'm flying. Drifting on the wind.

Yellow rays split through gray clouds to bathe her in warmth. Wide dunes passed beneath her, like still waves of a sandy sea.

A man knelt on top of one of the hills. A fleck of red shimmered in his black hair. Warrenna watched as he fell onto his back, clutching his right leg, gasping for air.

She didn't want to watch the man suffer anymore. Those hills didn't feel like home anyway. But she knew she would be there soon.

She let the wind carry her away from the thunder in the distance....

The sandy hills were endless. Every step brought pain to his leg, and nothing he did would lessen it. The fire in his lungs stole his breath.

Sacred Mount Zeraphet was not yet on the horizon. Was he to die among these low hills, his eyes never gazing upon Zeraphet's skies? Would he wander the land as a restless spirit because he was not strong enough to complete his journey?

He fell to his knees. He willed himself to get up, to stumble forward, but his breath would not come. He fell onto his back.

A gray hawk passed overhead, but quickly shrank to a tiny speck as it climbed out of sight.

And then he heard footsteps.

A woman wearing a thin doeskin wrap climbed the hill.

She was small, and the black braid over her shoulder reached her waist.

Again he tried to stand, and again he could not. "Leave me alone," he said.

Mother-to-Doves stopped before him and pointed to the west. "The healing waters of Telikiva Stream are just beyond that pass. The touch of the River-God will restore your strength."

He shook his head. "I will not make it. I will die in these hills. And if you stay, the evil spirit I carry will overcome you."

"You will make it. I will help you."

He sneered. "The teachings say the warrior must complete the journey on his own. You would have me defy the ways of our ancestors?"

"The teachings say nothing of the venom you carry." She pointed to the sun. "The Sky-God has watched every step you have taken. The courage you have shown in these days honors Her. Now honor Her again. Let me help you."

She extended her hand. "Do you want to see the skies of Zeraphet or not?"

Thomas focused on the dotted yellow line as he drove, determined not to drift away again and repeat yesterday's embarrassing hallway awakening. But it wasn't easy. The pain in Warrenna's eyes and the resignation in her voice kept returning to mind.

"The more time you spend with me, the more danger you put yourself in."

What was happening? What was she afraid of?

He made a point of waving and saying hi to his friends as he walked to the spot where he woke the previous day. Even though he waited past the first bell, he didn't see Warrenna. He wasn't planning to confront her at first. A hello, a smile, and a "How are ya?" were all he wanted to give. He would pursue the danger question later. But she didn't show up.

After first hour, he patrolled the art hallway where he saw her the day before. But the only person there was a tall man with a short white beard. His white linen suit was hard to miss as he slowly walked by the classrooms.

So she's not at school today. I hope she's all right.

As Thomas drifted across campus toward his second-hour class, he began to feel hopeless, like every decision he made was futile and irrelevant. He wondered why he should bother finishing the day at school.

Thomas bit deep into his cheek and chided himself for being stupid. No matter how much he wanted to, he couldn't do anything about Warrenna just then. There were only so many days left before high school ended and his friends spread out around the country. He couldn't waste them feeling sad for no reason.

It's time to be me again.

He pulled open the door to his second-hour business law class and winked at the first pretty girl he saw.

One hour of good-natured teacher-torture later, Thomas felt better, and he looked forward to another fun hour ahead of him in English. As he entered Mrs. Hayes's room, he glanced toward the corner. Warrenna wasn't there, but he got an idea. He could take his notes to her after practice. That would provide an opportunity to ask her what danger he was in.

Inspired by his sharp thinking, Thomas made his way to his desk as he had most every day before this strange week, with a clear head and a silly grin.

He spotted his friends and said, "'Sup, C-Rod?"

"Nuthin', man," Corwyn replied. "Psyched for Sunnyslope this weekend. It'll help me forget about last week's game."

"Yeah, we take care of the ball and keep feedin' the big guy, and we'll be set. Isn't that right, B?"

Brendan scratched his chin and yawned. "Yeah. Just can't lose our heads. Or let cheerleaders distract us." He smiled at Corwyn, then looked hard at Thomas for a quick moment. "How you doin'?" Brendon's question was amiable, but his look was serious.

Thomas returned Brendan's look with a speedy *everything's-cool* nod. "I'm good. Real good. You still want me to look at your Lawrence paper before you turn it in?"

"Yeah, if you can."

"Get a draft to me Monday, I'll get it back to you Tuesday, and you can work on the changes over the week."

Brendan nodded. "Sounds good. Thanks."

Thomas spotted Mariah's trademark golden hair as she entered the room. He smiled at her.

"Hey, lady."

"Hey yourself, Tommy. How are ya?"

Her words were casual, but her eyes were steady and grave. Thomas couldn't help but feel flattered by his friends' concern. "Good," he said. "Doin' real good."

"Happy to hear it." She smiled at him.

Thomas didn't have any quick comeback, but that didn't matter just then, not while those eyes sparkled at him.

"Hey, guys," Brendan said. "Janey's cookin' up some kinda after-game party at her father's place on Saturday. Sounds like there's gonna be a ton of people there. You guys wanna come?"

Thomas jumped at the opportunity: "Sure, sounds like fun." He looked at Mariah. "If *you're* interested."

"I'm interested," she said with a sly smile. "Should be a good party. Sweet Jane's daddy lets his little girl do just about anything to stay in her good graces. Pick me up?"

"Sure. I'll need to get cleaned up after the game."

"But Tommy, you *know* how much I love riding in cars with sweaty, smelly boys."

They laughed. Class began, and after a few minutes, Mariah passed him a note:

Feel like telling me what was really *bothering you yesterday?*

Thomas smirked, then decided that one of the reasons he liked Mariah was her directness.

He wrote back, *Was it that obvious?*

I don't know who was sitting behind me, but it wasn't you. Want to talk about it?

Thomas chewed on his cheek as he stared at Mariah's flowery script. She deserved honesty, but the truth was complicated and embarrassing.

Thinking too much, he finally wrote. *Worrying about the future, all the things I'm going to do for the first time. Like finding a place to live and taking care of it, paying bills, getting used to a new town, handling college classes, etc. It's all a little too much.*

Her response took a few minutes to return.

I know what you mean. We're going from a place with a routine we've had for four years, to a place with new challenges every day. Like avoiding the extra freshman 15 pounds and wondering if your little cousin will hate you for moving away. (OK, maybe that's just me.) But aren't you psyched to get out of your house?

His reply took a while, too. *I suppose. I think what I'm really dreading is losing all my friends. Like Brendan. He's going to LA. I'm going to Maldecido. I guess I'll see him when we're both back in B-Ville. But how often will that be? Christmas, and maybe spring break?*

This time, Mariah's response came back quickly. *The friendships don't end, they just change. They'll only end if you want them to. And you'll make lots of new friends at SAU. You're really easy to like.*

Thomas glowed at that. *Thanks,* he wrote back. *I guess I just really like where I am now and don't want it to end.*

Mariah tapped the note when she passed it back. *It's NOT going to end. You're going to build on it. You'll do fine. You're sharp, and not the type of jerk who's afraid to ask someone when he isn't sure what to do. Plus, I'll be at SAU with you. Us B-Villers look out for each other.*

Thomas grinned. He didn't know where his relationship with Mariah would be when it came time to move to the big city. But he wasn't concerned. They would take on the newness together.

As for now, it didn't matter that she didn't know about his strange sadness of the past few days, or about the dreams he'd had every night of his life. Her ignorance wouldn't hurt either of them.

The empty desk in the corner pulled at Thomas's gaze, and he couldn't help but wonder where Warrenna was. Then he scoffed at himself for worrying. It was probably nothing.

Shifting red shapes, blurry edges that pulsed when she looked at them.

And thirst. Profound thirst, beginning deep in Warrenna's stomach and burning every inch of her throat as it clawed its way through her mouth, her nose, even her eyes.

Eventually Warrenna realized that her eyes were closed. The red blobs were actually moving across the underside of her eyelids.

She lay on her back, tucked into a soft bed. Thick pillows propped her head up.

Warrenna felt Alexandria's form beside her, above the covers. After a moment, Warrenna could make out the dark blankets tacked to the wall to conceal the windows. This was her parents' bedroom. But why was she here? And why was she so *thirsty*?

Alexandria gently stroked her daughter's forehead, the same way she did when Warrenna was a child.

"Can you hear me?"

Warrenna tried to say yes, but her throat locked up, and her lungs felt like empty soda bottles with the caps screwed on. She was only able to nod.

Alexandria smiled. "Good. You're going to be okay. Aunt Tammy is on her way."

The name sounded familiar, and after a moment, Warrenna remembered that Aunt Tammy was her personal doctor. Though not a familial relative, she had known Aunt Tammy most of her life. In hindsight, Warrenna knew that was because Aunt Tammy knew the most about Warrenna's condition.

That condition being the curse, which was the reason she hungered for the blood of others, and the reason she had no choice in how to live her life.

Warrenna remembered the bathroom, the razor, the burning in her arm. Tears filled her gray eyes, and the thirst burned even more.

I failed. I'm stuck with this life, this body, this bad blood. Only now, my parents know I'm not afraid to end it. I'll never get another chance.

And then she saw the dark marble inside her, in the place where the craving came from.

Only it wasn't a marble anymore. Now it was a sphere the size of a grapefruit, and solid, like steel.

Black and orange tentacles shot from the center of the pulsing mass, wrapping themselves around her heart, strangling what remained of her humanity.

Her head jerked back into the pillow. *Oh God, I'm turning!*

An image sprang into sight. She saw a pretty girl in the

cheerleading uniform, the same girl she passed in the hallway. There were Warrenna's powerful hands, keeping the girl still as she buried her fangs in the girl's neck. The prey whimpered pitifully; her taste was young and pure, and it was wonderful.

A sob choked out of Warrenna's burning throat. *Oh, God, no! I've forced my parents to kill me!*

Alexandria shushed her and kissed her tears. "You're all right, Renna. You're not going to turn. I'll get you something for the thirst in just a moment. But right now, you need to listen to me."

Warrenna felt her father's rough hand take her own. He stood on the other side of the bed, and his eyes were shining.

"You're much stronger than you think," Alexandria said. "You can already survive so much. But you'll feel lost and angry until you allow Zera into your life. She will quiet that storm in your heart, and guide you to peace and fulfillment. Forget about the great things we keep saying you're going to do. They aren't important. *You* are what's important, you and your tranquility. And you must believe me when I say that Zera is the only way. Every other road leads you to this bed, or to a prison, or to your own destruction."

Alexandria kissed Warrenna's forehead and wiped her tear-soaked cheeks with her thumb. "We love you, Renna," she whispered. "We want you to be happy, and so we're going to do everything we can to convince you to turn to Zera."

She ran a hand through her daughter's hair and sighed. "I'll get your medication now." She rose from the bed and left the room.

For a while, Warrenna kept her mouth closed as she wept. "How?" she gasped to Richard.

"I checked the bathroom door after about twenty minutes. When you didn't answer, I broke it down. I was trying to fix it just now."

That explains the thunder in the dream. She saw the sandy hills again, but the pain drenched her vision in deep crimson. She shivered, and her father squeezed her hand.

A tear slipped down Richard's cheek. "Renna, I really *am* sorry. I didn't want it like this. No one should ever be born with this curse. But Zera has done so much for us, and everything she's asked us to do has helped us survive. I have to trust that there's a good reason for this. One that doesn't sacrifice your happiness."

Warrenna was too ashamed to look at him as he continued. "All right, I know your mother's a little fanatical, okay? But she's absolutely right about this. You need a relationship with Zera, or else you'll be overwhelmed by what you are. Zera may be cold, but she's wise, and without her cleansings, I'd be a monster. I know you can't really see that there's a good reason why she brought you into this world. But you have to trust that there is one. It's either that, or go crazy."

It's too late, Dad. Can't you see? I'm already crazy.

Alexandria returned with a tall glass filled with a warm, bubble-gum-pink fluid. She instructed Warrenna to drink it all. The liquid was sweet and thick, and it dulled the pain in Warrenna's throat.

"Now rest," Alexandria said. "Your strength will return quickly, faster than you think."

Warrenna knew that medicine. As a child, she called it the Last Resort. When nothing else cured her stomachaches, she got a teaspoon of the cotton candy-flavored medicine. Now, she knew that the sugar masked the wonderful taste of human blood.

I wonder whose it was? I took so much. Will I need cleansings now?

Suddenly Warrenna's eyelids were heavy, and the bed was slowly sinking into the floor. The soft sheets gave way to wrap around her, surround her, enfold her.

Before she slipped away, she heard the low, urgent voices of her parents.

"We call you, oh, Zera, most holy and wise. Cleanse the craving from the blood of our holy daughter."

* * *

Even, shapeless white surrounded Warrenna, like she lay in the middle of a semi-solid cloud. She heard a rushing sound, like a far-off waterfall.

She saw nothing, but she could smell a whiff of ground black pepper.

"Zera."

A woman slowly appeared in the blankness. Black, twinkling eyes in a shadowless, porcelain face, flowing dark hair, like swooping ravens. She wore a long dark dress whose fabric shimmered faintly, like the midnight desert sky, and whose edges dissolved to smoke as they touched the boundless white.

"Hello, daughter. It has been a long time since you saw me."

Warrenna didn't say anything. The tips of Zera's dress curled, dissipated and reappeared, like dozens of tiny black flames.

"You probably don't remember," Zera's deep voice continued, "but your last cleansing was four years ago. It doesn't seem right. I see you every time you dream, yet you only see me when you are in pain."

Warrenna smirked. "I'm just lucky, I guess."

Zera extended her hand, a mere outline of flawless white in the blankness. She reached to Warrenna's shoulder, but Warrenna backed away.

"Can we just get this over with?"

The goddess frowned. "I can be quite useful, daughter. I've been watching humans for a long time, I know a lot about what they do. I hate to see you in pain."

"I don't care what you hate. I don't care if I ever see you again. You made me like this. I will never, *ever* forgive you for that."

Zera folded her arms, the outlines of white vanishing into the twinkling darkness of her dress. "There are reasons, good reasons that you would not understand."

"Yeah, I'm sure they're good for *you!*"

Zera sighed and raised a pale arm. A black hourglass, about the size of a shoebox, appeared in her left hand.

"Close your eyes, daughter. This will hurt."

The hourglass turned over, and for every grain of red sand that fell, a new fire ignited in Warrenna's blood.

Follow the chain.

Thomas darted through the forest of sweaty young men, keeping Corwyn's thin silver necklace in the center of his vision as he chased his friend back and forth under the basket.

Keep moving your feet. Don't over-pursue. Watch the screener.

Corwyn snaked through his teammates, to the left of one, then to the right of another, cutting close enough to rub shoulders with them. Thomas followed right behind, keeping his eyes on the silver line above his friend's practice jersey.

Near the sideline, he saw Corwyn's hands come up as though ready to catch the ball. Thomas had an opportunity to swat at where the ball was coming from, but he didn't.

The ball never came, and Corwyn immediately plunged back into the grove of players. Thomas didn't go for the fake, so he kept up with him.

Bright orange flickered in the corner of his eye. Thomas turned to look, and then crashed to the hardwood floor. His ears rang, and pain thumped in his jaw.

A whistle blew, and a half-dozen concerned faces peered down at him.

"Whoa, *dude*, are you all right?" Owes, the backup center, rubbed his elbow as he stood above Thomas.

Thomas wiggled his jaw. *What just happened?* "Uh, I think so."

"You gotta pay attention to where you are."

Coach Reeves had yelled the warning to the entire team. His leathery face moved to each of the panting players as he barked, "You can get hurt out here, ladies!"

Thomas sat up and rubbed his neck. There was no doubt: that had been Warrenna standing in the bleachers. And she was on fire.

The stands were empty now, but he remembered the vision clearly. Orange flames roared up from her feet, immersing her entire body. Her face was clenched in pain, but her mouth was closed even though she was burning alive. She wasn't crying out for help or screaming in agony. She wasn't even fighting it.

"You all right, son?"

There was no sympathy in Coach Reeves's shouted question. Sweat glistened on his bald head as he stood over his stunned player.

"Yeah," Thomas said. He scrambled to his feet. "I mean yes, sir. I still got all my teeth, sir."

"C'mere a minute, son."

Coach Reeves led Thomas away from the rest of the team, who now sprinted to the half-court line and back.

Reeves put a sweaty hand on the back of Thomas's neck. His breath reeked of cigarettes. "Listen, Gelbaugh, I don't know what's happened to you these last two practices, but I need you to get your head back in the game. You're an important part of this team. These boys, especially the younger kids, they're influenced by how much you hustle and how hard you work, playing-time or no playing-time."

"I know, sir. I'll be ready on Saturday, sir. You can count on it."

Reeves stared at his player, his dark eyes serious. "Yeah, you better be," he mumbled. Then he grinned. "Now get out there and run some suicides with your teammates."

"Yes, sir."

Thomas sprinted as hard as he could, and his burning lungs

reminded him of the fire consuming Warrenna. He wondered why she didn't appear to be struggling against the flames.

C'mon Tommy. Keep your head in the game.

And for the next hour, he fought to do just that.

Chapter 7

Thomas cruised south on Highway 20 beneath the Milky Way cloud of stars that reached from one horizon to the next in a wide sky-stripe. The black mountains swallowed up his headlights, and the engine's hum sounded muted, far away. The quiet privacy made it easy to think.

And what he thought about was Warrenna. Her vague warning of danger was followed by her absence at school, and then the strange vision of her burning body. A fire that high in the mountains would surely have spread to the forest, and he hadn't seen any smoke rising from the south.

But what if she wasn't at home when the fire started? She could be anywhere. But Thomas knew of only one place to look.

He turned his car onto Burnham Peak Road. After a few minutes, he recognized the clearing where he turned the car around on Wednesday. That led him to the dirt road where Warrenna had walked away from him.

There were no street lights, and tall trees blocked out most of the moonlight, so Thomas slowly advanced into the darkness.

The road was rocky and narrow as he gradually descended, and Thomas wondered what he would do if he reached a dead end. There wasn't enough room to turn around, and he didn't like the idea of attempting to back his way up the trail.

But the rutted tire tracks in the dust gave him hope that the road was used fairly often.

Something dashed across the road, and Thomas slammed on the brakes. A coyote stood before the car, his tiny eyes aglow with the reflected yellow headlights. The animal stared at Thomas for a moment, then snorted and disappeared into the forest.

His heartbeat thudded in his ears. *This is stupid. I should put the car in reverse right now.*

But he had come this far. And he wouldn't have a chance to return in the daytime until after the game on Saturday. And then there was the party afterward.

Figuring it couldn't be too much farther, Thomas released the brake. The car resumed its downward roll.

And then light exploded all around him.

Thomas slammed on the brakes again, squinting his eyes almost shut. *Now what?*

As his eyes became accustomed to the brightness, he was able to see a series of big lamps in the trees on either side of the road. Darkness remained behind him, but ahead of him, the road extended another twenty yards, then ended before a large two-story house.

The flat-roofed building looked like a brick. A few tiny windows peered out from the face, but mud-colored curtains blocked each of the openings from the inside. The exterior stucco was a similar shade of dirt. Pine trees surrounded the house on every side but the front.

A concrete driveway extended from the garage, and Thomas brought his car to a stop there and got out. It was funny, the closer he walked to the house, the darker the area became. When he reached the front door, the floodlights looked like ordinary streetlights.

Thomas practiced what he was going to say, then rang the doorbell. After a moment, the door was opened by a man with short dark hair and a dark, close-trimmed goatee. The belt of his purple bathrobe was tightly knotted around the hips of his lean frame. Thomas wondered if the man was Renna's father. He looked too young.

The man didn't say anything. His hazel eyes simply stared. He didn't look angry, but he was definitely not smiling.

Thomas fought the urge to run. "Uh, hi. My name's Thomas. I'm a friend of Renna's and I noticed she wasn't at school today. I, uh, thought maybe she'd want a copy of the notes I took in English. I couldn't find a phone number, and since I dropped her off yesterday I sort of knew where she, uh, where you and she live. Uh, assuming that you, uh, live here, and aren't just, you know, visiting?"

The man rubbed the dark rings beneath his eyes and held out a pale hand. "I'll make sure Warrenna gets your notes."

Thomas's own hand trembled as he raised the two scribbled pages and offered them to the man.

"Is Renna okay?"

"Yes, she's just a little sick." Each of the man's words was carefully pronounced, but Thomas heard no accent.

"Father? May I speak to my friend outside for a moment?"

Warrenna stood behind the man, rubbing her neck. A thin, olive-drab sweater hung on her bony arms, and her hair was pulled away from her pale face. She stared steadily at the man she called "Father," as though daring him to say no.

Thomas had dealt with scowling fathers before, but something about this one made him not want to say or do anything to win him over. Warrenna and the man held the stare for so long Thomas considered making a break for his car and getting the heck out of there.

"Very well," the man finally said. "Don't go too far."

"Thank you, Father." Warrenna turned her gray eyes onto Thomas as she walked past the man.

She didn't slow down as she glided past Thomas, too. "Walk with me, won't you, Thomas?"

It took Thomas a couple of strides to catch up to her as she made a beeline for the Beatermobile.

"I thought I told you to leave me alone."

"I-I was just bringing you the notes. You're welcome."

She looked up to the night sky and shook her head. "Notes. You don't have any idea what kind of danger you've put yourself in by coming here."

"You're right, I don't have any idea. What kind of danger? From who? Your parents?"

"No, you idiot." She finally looked at him. "From *me!*"

Thomas stopped, but Warrenna kept walking until the Beatermobile stood between her and the front door.

"I don't understand," he said. "What do you mean?"

Warrenna just shook her head and covered her eyes with her hand.

"Listen," Thomas said, "all I know is that something's wrong, something's really bothering you, I can, well, I can just feel it. I'm worried about you."

Warrenna lowered her hand and glared at him. "I'm not the one you need to be worried about."

"Then who is?"

"You are, you numbskull!" She winced and glanced back toward the house, then lowered her voice and pointed to the road behind him. "Just get the hell out of here while you still can."

"Tell me why!" Thomas didn't care that he was yelling now. "Just tell me that and I'll leave you right now and never speak to you again. Just tell me why."

Warrenna grinned, her eyes wild. "Fine. I'll do you one better, Thomas. I'll *show* you why."

She stepped away from him and tilted her head back. Her shoulders twitched, her sides convulsed and her eyes rolled about in circles. A choking gasp escaped her throat, as though she were trying to vomit up a live cat.

The shaking continued for a couple of achingly slow seconds. Warrenna's grunts were swallowed into the silent forest around them. When the tremors finally stopped, Warrenna hunched her shoulders and dropped her chin to her chest. Her breathing became a deep, regular wheeze, and she slowly lifted her eyes to Thomas.

Her gray irises were gone, replaced by pulsing crimson. Her pupils were narrow, vertical slits of black. She barred her teeth, revealing two sets of inch-long canine fangs, and slowly fanned her hooked talons mere inches from his face.

"You see?" she grunted. Her voice was a low, raw rasp. *"This* is why you should be afraid of me."

Thomas watched the changes in numb amazement, wondering if he was dreaming. There she was, looking for all the world like a vampire!

And then each of the strange, gloomy feelings he experienced in the past week resurfaced. He felt them all again, one after the other, until they combined into an overpowering sorrow. But the feeling was warm. It glowed comfortably in his chest.

This must be why I've been so sad around her and why she kept telling me to stay away. It's so obvious. Why didn't I think of this before? She's a vampire, and no one in their right mind would want to be.

His eyes were wet with familiar tears. But this time, warmth spread to his arms and legs. "Oh, Warrenna. I'm so sorry."

The beast frowned in confusion. "You're not afraid?"

"No." The words came easily, like he wanted to say them for a long time. "No, I'm not afraid. I know you won't hurt me."

She leaned closer and licked her fangs with a forked purple tongue. "How can you be sure, little man? Maybe I would really *like* hurting you."

Thomas shrugged. "I don't really know why I'm not afraid of you. But I know where all of my tears have come from now." He wiped his streaming face. "You're cursed, and that makes me sad. But I'm not scared. I know you wouldn't hurt me, or anyone for that matter. It's not in you. Am I right?"

Warrenna sputtered and gestured to her mouth. "Not *in* me? I'm a monster. I can tear you apart in a heartbeat. I can suck you dry within a minute."

Thomas placed his hand on her shoulder. Her sweater was hot to the touch, but he didn't recoil.

"Renna, something's happening to me. It has something to do with you. Maybe with my dreams, too. But you've been clear about not wanting anything to do with me. So if you can tell me that nothing special is happening to you because of me, then I'll go. Get back in my car, drive home, go to sleep, and forget I ever met you. Your secret will be safe. You can trust me."

Warrenna bowed her head. When she looked back up, her gray eyes returned, the canines withdrew, and the claws retracted. She stared at him with her jaw hung open in astonishment.

Thomas sniffled. "Well?"

Warrenna looked at her small, now-human hands and shook her head. "Unbelievable," she whispered. "Yeah, I fight the curse, like my parents do. So we don't hurt anyone. Somehow you knew that."

He moved closer to her. "But do you feel any different? Being around me?"

She looked at him. The floodlights sparkled in her watery eyes like stars shining through a cloudy night. "That morning when you apologized to me, I felt relieved. Like I'd finally found something. Something safe. But more than that, when I'm around you, I forget."

"Forget? What do you forget?"

A tear rolled down her pale cheek. "I forget that I'm a vampire."

Thomas smiled. *Am I sure I'm not dreaming?*

"So," he said. "Um, what do you think is happening here?"

Warrenna spread her arms out and shrugged her shoulders. "I have no idea. But you're not scared of me, and that makes me really happy." She rubbed her bandaged wrist. "I haven't been happy in a long time."

"Warrenna?" The man's voice boomed from the front door.

She glanced back at the door and backed away. "I have to go, but I will see you tomorrow. Here, after seven? Please come."

"Of course," Thomas said loud enough for anyone to hear. "Good night, Renna."

She smiled at him, wiped at the tears, and skipped back to the door.

Thomas climbed into the Beatermobile, barely feeling the seat beneath him, or the wheel in his hands. Maybe there *was* such a thing as fate. Maybe fate had brought him into the depths of Tebon Canyon to see what he saw, to say what he said.

He carefully drove back up the dirt road, and reached the Highway 20 stop sign. He clicked the turn signal on.

Wait a minute. Did I really just talk to a vampire?

Chapter 8

Thomas rubbed his eyes and read over the sloppy words one more time. There was nothing in his journal about Tebon Canyon, a bright dirt road, or whatever Warrenna had turned into.

And so, for the first time, Thomas was sure he didn't dream about a vampire.

The clock buzzed, but Thomas was lost in the sorrow that overwhelmed him when he saw those scarlet eyes. The sadness felt comfortable, as though it was the most natural and appropriate response to what he saw.

But that made no sense. *I didn't even believe in vampires until last night. How could I be comfortable with Renna being one?*

Two emotions emerged as his alarm continued its whine.

Naturally, he was scared. Warrenna and her parents were vampires, or something that looked like the monsters in the movies. Some form of the legendary creatures truly did exist, and probably hunted people for food. What's more, she walked through the Chiricahua parking lot with him in the sun. *So much for the old myths*. He wondered what else was out there stalking humans like him. Did he have to worry about ghosts, demons and werewolves now? *I'm never leaving the house again.*

The unbidden thought made him chuckle, because Thomas was also excited. He couldn't wait to see Warrenna again, to find out more about what she was and why he wasn't afraid of her. He remembered the tingly feeling in his eyes, and the way his words came so easily. He wanted to feel that way again, so confident, so energized.

It's like I've been half-asleep all my life, and finally woke up all the way last night. For a little while, anyway.

He wondered what, if anything, his dreams had to do with all this.

He touched the snooze button to silence his alarm. There was more to think about before he showered. He didn't want his memories of last night to melt away in the water like his dreams did.

He wanted to go see Warrenna right then, after a shower, and breakfast, and probably after brushing his teeth. He guessed he would be safe at her house. She could protect him. She had to know about all the supernatural stuff out there.

But she asked him to come over in the evening, and he had to honor that. So what could he do in the meantime? Going to school felt like a joke. He could never learn anything important there. And it was Friday, a perfect day to skip.

Thomas bolted upright. *People will notice if I stay home. The school will call, then my parents will ask me what happened, and more questions will follow.*

He found his pile of clothes and dashed to the shower. *I gotta act normal. Gotta keep her secret. Warrenna's life might depend it.*

And that meant going to school as if nothing strange happened last night.

* * *

Warrenna gently dabbed the size four brush into the puddle of acrylic paint and held its head to the canvas. She blended the orange around the horizon, brightening the painting's outline and giving the landscape a larger, more expansive feeling.

More attention on the sunset for what it is, not for the night that threatens it.

She took a step back. *Homecoming* was giving her that rare right feeling, like the images were pouring directly from her imagination onto the canvas. It reminded her of the feeling Tommy gave her last night. Belonging.

She touched her cheek to her shoulder. *He saw what I really am, and he wasn't afraid.*

She shifted her focus to the man in the center of the painting. The sunset was in the background, but she wanted his form to be more than just a shadowy blur. She decided to rotate the perspective a tiny bit.

There was a knock on her open door. Leaning in from the hall was a smooth face wearing small spectacles with bright orange lenses.

"Hey, Renna."

"Oh. Hey, Aunt Tammy."

"You got a sec?"

"Depends. Got good news?"

"Sort of." Aunt Tammy dragged a stool up to Warrenna's easel and perched herself on it. "How are you feeling?"

"Kinda tired." Warrenna looked back to the painting. "I slept really well last night. I can't remember the last time I slept that hard."

Aunt Tammy nodded. "You put yourself through quite an ordeal, and your body needs to recover." She ran her index fingers through her black hair to hook the locks under her ears. "How about the craving?"

Warrenna froze. She hadn't pictured the marble since Thomas left. It was still beneath her heart, hard, inescapable. But it wasn't as dark.

"I haven't felt the craving all morning," she said. She looked back at Aunt Tammy. "It was so overwhelming yesterday."

"Yeah, that's pretty strange for it to vanish like that. Wanna hear something else strange?"

Warrenna smirked. "I dunno. Do I?"

Aunt Tammy drummed her fingers on the underside of the stool and rocked her small frame from side to side. "I think you want to hear it. Your uncle Vince just gave me your test results from this morning. You know those hook-cells I told you about?"

"The dirt in our blood. That's the stuff you measure to get a rough idea of how badly someone is affected by our curse."

"Pretty much. So, Vin tells me your hook-cell count is actually lower than the last sample we took two weeks ago."

"Lower?" Warrenna blinked. "You'd think it'd be higher, right?"

"Yes, I'd think." Aunt Tammy folded her arms. "When people like us lose a couple pints of blood and survive, the levels get higher. Just like if we taste living human blood. The craving gets worse, so we need cleansings more frequently, and the cycle continues. Your parents performed the ritual in a timely manner, but your levels should be higher after all that happened. Not lower."

Warrenna grinned. "I've always been bad at math. Maybe my blood is too."

Suddenly Aunt Tammy sprang from the stool and grabbed Warrenna's smiling face by the chin. "Those marks on your gums," she growled, her nails pinching Warrenna's mouth open. "You've transformed."

She released Warrena's chin with a shove. "Oh, that's just fantastic! Why didn't your mother tell me about this?"

"I didn't do anything like that."

"You know better than to lie to me, Renna. If you do, how can I help you?"

Warrenna rubbed her bandaged wrist, feeling ashamed and small. "Okay," she mumbled. "It was last night, outside. I didn't tell anyone. Mom didn't tell you because she didn't know."

Aunt Tammy shook her head in disgust. "Ugh, Renna! That is so *dumb*. What if you were seen? What if you lost control and killed someone? You'd expose all of us."

"I know that."

"It'd be San Francisco all over again," Aunt Tammy continued. "That idiot Hank thought he'd blow off some steam by running in the hills in his other form, and do you know what happened? He was seen. And not only that, he was video-taped! We had to totally abandon our Northern California organization. There were infected people there, people that needed us, and thanks to that idiot they never got…"

She stopped in mid-rant, her entire body freezing in position. Then, with a quick swivel, Aunt Tammy turned away from Warrenna and chewed on the knuckle of her index finger.

"Wait a minute," she said, the anger gone. "You bled, were cleansed, and transformed. But still, your hook-level went down."

Warrenna rubbed her neck, relieved that Aunt Tammy had stopped yelling. "Maybe your test has a problem?"

Aunt Tammy shook her head and rubbed her pale hands on her sleek black pants. "Vince said he ran it three times." She sighed. "But I have to assume something went wrong. I'll get him up here. He'll have to take another sample."

"Can't you do it?"

Aunt Tammy smirked. "I'd rather not test my self-discipline. Blood is still blood. It's safest to have someone not afflicted with our curse do the procedure. Vince should still be in town. I'll go give him a ring right now."

She turned to go, stopped, and turned back, looking through

Patrick Vaughn

her bright orange lenses into Warrenna's eyes. "Unless there's something you're not telling me."

Warrenna looked away. She had no idea how her father would react to hearing that a human boy knew about her curse, other than that he would be furious. He might hunt down Thomas himself, for all Warrenna knew. It wouldn't matter that Thomas promised not to tell anyone.

Aunt Tammy's hand was on her shoulder. "I know something's up, Renna. You aren't acting like someone who just tried to end her life. You're entirely too happy. What's going on? Why'd you transform?"

Warrenna wouldn't look at her. It didn't matter if Thomas wasn't afraid of her true form. She had put him in terrible danger.

"You can tell me," Aunt Tammy said. "I won't be angry."

Warrenna turned and saw Aunt Tammy's patient smile. The same smile Warrenna remembered from Bellingham, and San Francisco, and Reno, when she asked her "aunt" all those questions she was too embarrassed to ask her mother. Aunt Tammy would touch her shoulder, peer through those orange glasses and patiently explain why Warrenna's baby teeth were falling out, or how boys were different, or why the other girls bled for a few days every month.

Warrenna sighed again. *I have to tell her. But maybe I can convince her to leave Thomas alone.*

"This boy at school was acting weird around me, as if just being around me made him really sad. He even started crying in front of me. Anyway, he thinks my paintings and his dreams are connected somehow. I don't think they are, but he kept bothering me about it. He even came here last night.

"I told him to leave me alone, for his own good, but he wasn't having any of it. So, I kinda wanted to scare him, so I transformed. I didn't really mean to. It sort of happened on its own. But he wasn't scared. He didn't even look surprised, just sad. And then I changed back."

Warrenna's eyes brimmed with tears. "And I remember this feeling I got the second or third time I saw him. Like a whole mountain of worries were lifted away from my shoulders. It only lasted a moment, but last night I had it again, when I saw that he wasn't scared of what I really am. I had it the rest of the night. Woke up with it this morning."

She peered up into Aunt Tammy's face. "Maybe it's what let me sleep so well. And I can't wait to see him again. I don't really know why. My life isn't any different. I mean, I still have no control over how I'm going to live and what I'm going to do. But I like this feeling. I really, *really* like it."

Aunt Tammy smiled and gently pushed the hair away from Warrenna's gray eyes. "That's *amoré*."

"What?"

"Oh, nothing. Hmm." Aunt Tammy chewed on her knuckle. "You said he thinks his dreams and your paintings are connected?"

Warrenna sniffled. "Yeah. He said he dreams really vivid every night, and that he always has. And that he's never seen anyone he knows in them. He saw my painting on display at school, and he said it did something weird to him. Like he saw a different angle in the dream or something."

"Hmmm." Aunt Tammy stared at the floor, a small smile playing around the corners of her mouth.

"Aunt Tammy?"

"Mmm?"

"I asked him to come over tonight. You don't think my father will hurt him, do you?"

Aunt Tammy lifted her head and grinned. "No! No-no-no. No, I have a feeling that'd be really foolish."

"Why? Do you know something?"

"I know *lots* of things. But I've never heard of anything like what's happened with you and your friend."

"Really? Is that good?"

Aunt Tammy just smiled, tousled Warrenna's hair, and left the room.

Chapter 9

As Thomas walked up the concrete footpath to Warrenna's house, he realized the only sounds he could hear belonged to him. His quick breath, his shuffling feet, his beating heart. Even though he stood in the midst of a forested canyon, he didn't hear any crickets, birds, or rodents. He just heard himself.

He reached the ordinary brown door and tucked his latest dream-journal under his sweater. As he lifted his finger to ring the doorbell, an icy breeze blew into his back. The chill ran up his spine, into his neck and down his arms.

Maybe this is a mistake. Vampires were waiting for him behind this door. He thought about coming back tomorrow, or maybe Sunday. Yes, a weekend, during the day, when it was warmer, easier to see, and probably harder for vampires to rip out his throat.

The more he considered leaving, the better it sounded. But just as he turned to go, the door opened.

Thomas quickly turned back to see the man with the goatee standing in the doorway. Today he wore black slacks and a white dress shirt without a tie. His smile didn't reach his eyes.

"Ah, Thomas. We've been expecting you. Won't you come in?"

Like before, the man said his words slowly, each syllable carefully pronounced. His strange speech made Thomas even more apprehensive. But he thought of Warrenna again, and how certain he was that she would never hurt him. Surely that feeling applied to her parents as well. At least he hoped so.

"Thank you, sir," Thomas said, and stepped inside.

The man led him through a narrow hallway to a wide room with a vaulted ceiling. The room glowed with dim orange light from fixtures set into the wall, like torches in some medieval castle. Beside the lamps hung dozens of framed sketches of an hourglass rising above outlines of flame. The identical drawings formed a line at eye-level along each wall. Though Thomas looked to be neck-deep in a pit of fire, the room was so cold that he expected a layer of frost to develop on his skin.

As his eyes adjusted to the dimness, Thomas saw that the room was actually two stories high. In the corner, a staircase ascended to a second, elevated level, like a cabin's loft. He wondered if the occupants of the house slept hanging upside down beneath the platform, and fought a sudden chuckle.

The room had no windows. *Of course it doesn't.*

"I apologize for my rudeness last night," the man said. "I was a bit tired, and not expecting guests." He extended his hand. "My name is Richard Dennison. I'm Warrenna's father. It's nice to meet you."

Thomas shook his hand: firm, normal. "Same here, sir. My name's Thomas Gelbaugh."

"Yes, Thomas, I know."

"Huh? Oh. Right."

Richard gestured to an easy chair covered in black leather. The seat was comfortable, but cold when Thomas lowered himself into it. The vampire sat in a huge black leather couch just to the side of Thomas.

"You know, Thomas," Richard began, "my daughter did something unusual this afternoon. She *talked* to us. She told her mother and me all about you, and about what you discovered last night. So tell me. Are you frightened?"

Richard's face was blank, so Thomas couldn't tell if the vampire was joking. "Uh, no sir. A little nervous, but no, not frightened."

Richard's dark eyebrows arched. "Don't you think you *should* be frightened? As far as you know, you've entered the lair of at least three vampires. I think that should frighten you. That should frighten anyone."

"Well, I'm not scared of Warrenna, sir. I know she'd never hurt me. It, uh, follows that her parents wouldn't hurt me either."

Richard's blank stare sent an itch burning down Thomas's spine. The vampire slowly rubbed his palms together. "You should be careful what you assume, young man. Sometimes apples fall far from the tree. Sometimes they roll down hills."

Thomas clenched his fists, but his arms still quivered from Richard's cold face. He took a deep breath. "Have I assumed incorrectly, sir?"

"Stay away from my daughter."

"Sir?"

"I think you heard me."

Thomas squirmed under the vampire's emotionless voice. "But why?"

"Because you are bad for her, Thomas. Yesterday, my daughter deliberately hurt herself, and then transformed in front of a human. I think you are the reason both of these events occurred."

Thomas remembered the bandage on Warrenna's wrist. Was it the result of a suicide attempt? Could he have somehow driven her to it? But then why was she smiling when she left him? Why did she skip to the front door?

"Out of respect for my daughter, I'm not going to hurt you. I know you're not stupid enough to share my family's secret, so I'm just going to forbid you from seeing her and leave it at that."

The vampire stood and gestured to the door. "If you care about Warrenna, you will understand and go without making a scene."

Thomas ground the flesh of his cheeks between his teeth and remained seated. "I disagree, sir. I don't think I'm bad for Warrenna. And I think she'll say the same thing, if you ask her."

"And I think you two are both too young to see through your naïveté. You should remember that I have far more experience in dealing with our affliction than you do. I know what's good and what's bad when I see it. Now, please leave my home."

"I'll go," Thomas said as he stood, "but you're going to have to leave town to keep me from seeing Warrenna every day at school."

Richard didn't react, and Thomas kept his gaze steady on the vampire's cold eyes. "With all respect, sir, there's something between your daughter and me. And I'm going to find out what it is. No one is going to keep me from doing that. Not you, not anyone."

Thomas regretted his words as soon as he closed his mouth. Richard's eyes flashed and his lips contorted into a snarl.

"How dare you," he growled. "How dare you defy me in my own home!"

Thomas tried to make a break for the door, but his legs refused to move. Then his lungs stiffened, preventing him from even drawing a breath.

Richard took a step toward him. Thomas's stomach folded in on itself. *This is it. I'm going to die.* He pictured the vampire's fangs tearing into his neck, his dark blood splattering onto the creamy carpet.

Richard's snarl quivered, and, in the blink of an eye, his lips squirmed to a tight grin. Then Thomas heard a soft blowing noise. He realized the vampire was laughing.

No, he was *giggling*.

Richard's eyes were wet with suppressed laughter, and he had trouble catching his breath. "Had you going there, huh?"

Thomas could only stare. Imaginary fangs were still deep in his jugular, sucking away his life.

"I must apologize for my husband. He has an odd sense of humor."

Thomas turned to find a pale, slender woman standing in a dark archway. She had a smooth oval face, and her auburn hair, so like Warrenna's, fell easily to her shoulders. She wore a fuzzy black sweater and a tight gray skirt that hugged her legs all the way down to the carpet.

The woman smiled, and her dark eyes sparkled. "Hello, Thomas. My name is Alexandria. I'm Warrenna's mother."

Her voice was deep and soothing, like a lullaby. "I can see by your face that my husband has given you a bit of a shock. I'm sorry about that, but you must understand. When we put our trust in someone, we must know how that person will react when pressed. When the chips are down, as they say. You reacted with honesty and passion. That means a lot to us."

Thomas's wide eyes darted from one vampire to the other. Richard had finally stopped laughing, and was now grinning widely.

"So," Thomas said. "Uh. You *don't* think I'm bad for Warrenna?"

"Not at all," Richard said jovially. "In fact, we suspect the opposite."

"The opposite? You mean that I'm good for her?"

"That's what it looks like," Alexandria said. She touched his arm. Her fingers were frosty, even through his sweater. "If you'll come with me, we have some tests we need to run on you."

Thomas pulled his arm away. "No disrespect, ma'am, but I'm a little confused, and I just really want to see Warrenna before my head explodes."

"That sounds like it would be messy."

Warrenna stood on the landing across the room, leaning her elbows on the banister. Thomas could not guess how long she had been there, but he had never been happier to see anyone in his short life.

"Yeah, probably," he called back to her.

She gestured toward the hallway. "It's okay. Take the tests. There are some strange things about you that need investigating. It won't take long. I'm not going anywhere."

Thomas couldn't help but smile. "So I'm the strange one?"

"Strange is relative, young man," Alexandria said. "By being fully human, you *are* the strange one here. But there's obviously more going on with you than with most humans. I think you would agree?"

Thomas looked to Warrenna, who nodded.

He took a deep breath. "I do agree, ma'am. It's why I'm here."

Then he followed Alexandria into the darkness.

Good old 'Tides' You haven't changed a bit.

Warrenna lay on her bed, fiddling with the buttons of her shirt. Carefully tacked to the ceiling was an abstract painting she created a few years ago, back in Bellingham, back when her worries were limited to grades, shyness with boys, curfew, allowances, and so on. Green, blue, and black waves swirled and blended in a dizzying pattern designed to frustrate the eye. *Turning Tides* was supposed to convey her confusion, but the painting now brought her a sad sort of comfort, both relaxing and depressing.

Let's face it. Those inspirational problems are blissfully ordinary now.

She sighed, and the scent from her ginger incense tickled her nose. Aunt Tammy was certain the boy downstairs was somehow making the curse fade. But Thomas had no idea what kind of world he was stepping into.

"Hey."

He stood in the doorway holding his left arm at the elbow. He looked around her room in a stupor, like he was waking from a bewildering dream.

Warrenna didn't get up. "I see you met Aunt Tammy and Uncle Vince."

"Uh, yeah. What's with Tammy's glasses?"

She shrugged. "She says her eyes are even more sensitive than mine. How'd the testing go?"

"I don't know. They just took some blood and had me stare at a candle for a few minutes. They wouldn't answer any of my questions."

Warrenna sat up, her bony ankles dangling over the side of her bed. "You sure you want them answered?"

Thomas's bright eyes drifted from painting to painting, but not to Warrenna. "They said I'm good for you. Is it true?"

"They think so. It makes sense. I should be much worse after all the stuff I've done."

He looked at the thick bandage on her wrist, and she rubbed it self-consciously. His eyes darted to the collection of paper cranes on her chest-of-drawers.

"So," he said. "You've always, uh, been like this?"

Relieved that Thomas didn't inquire about her wound, Warrenna nodded and told him the truth. "My parents didn't tell me until three months ago, but yeah, I was born like this. My symptoms aren't nearly as bad as theirs, and they apparently slipped me blood whenever I got sick. Then there are the prayers, but you don't want to know about all that."

His stare moved to the ceiling, where his eyes spun in the swirls of *Turning Tides*. "But I saw you in the sun. Vampires aren't supposed to survive that."

"Being a vampire isn't an all-or-nothing condition for us. My parents found a way to make the curse like a disease. We can slow the transformation that occurs after someone gets infected. Normally, it takes ten days to lose your humanity. With our process, people can hold out for years without needing the blood of the living to survive. My mother and father can't be in the sun anymore, but I still can. For a while, anyway."

Thomas nodded, and finally looked into Warrenna's eyes. His gaze was steady, but his jaw was clenched. "So if it's a disease, then what's death?"

Warrenna searched his eyes, and guessed he was fighting his customary tears. "Let's see. Death is losing control of your urges, letting them control you. Sort of like last night, when the beast emerged. Allowing it to kill you would've been my death."

His eyes dropped to her bandaged wrist. She tucked her arm behind her back and looked away.

He took a step closer. "Is this a terminal disease?"

She nodded. "It's all borrowed time. The craving never stops growing. We all get a little worse with every passing week. Except me, apparently. Because of you."

He frowned. "You don't seem too happy about this. I mean you're looking at a potential cure for this terrible condition, and you don't even seem interested."

"There's too much I don't know. I mean, yeah, I feel good when we're together, but you obviously don't."

"You mean the tears? Now that I know what you are, I think I've got it under control. You don't see any now, do you?"

Warrenna rubbed her neck. Thomas was close enough now that she could hear his steady breathing. "Yeah, but think about it. When I'm around you, I get better. The evil in me is lessened. It goes away. But what happens to you? What if I'm taking something away from you to balance it out?"

Thomas squinted, so she added, "What if I'm taking away some of your holiness?"

"What, you think I'm an angel?" He grunted dismissively.

"Maybe. Or something like it. If there're things like me, there's probably things like angels."

Thomas chuckled. "I think I'd know if I were an angel."

Now it was Warrenna's turn to smile. "Oh, yeah? I didn't know I was a vampire for sixteen years."

Thomas shook his head, but then he clenched his jaw again and turned away. His steady breathing stopped, and his hand closed into a trembling fist.

"What?" Warrenna said. "What's wrong?"

Maybe I'm doing something to him right now. Maybe I'm sucking away some precious part of him to repair a tiny bit of my natural evil.

Thomas stuttered, then lifted his sweater. A thin notebook was wedged between his belt and his undershirt. Without turning toward her, he tossed the book at Warrenna.

"M-Monday, February t-twenty-f-fifth," he whispered. "I'm there. I'm there right now."

Warrenna could only see the whites of his half-closed eyes. "What do you mean?"

"Read."

The notebook was filled with wrinkled pages of scrawling ink. She found February 25th and quickly read about the end of a long journey, an incredible sunset over a desert, and an icy feeling in the heart.

Finally, Warrenna discovered that Thomas was looking at *Homecoming,* the painting with the man looking at a desert sunset from atop a cliff.

But now a soft white glow surrounded the canvas. The white light spread around the room, quietly washing out the carpet, her bed, and the paintings along the walls.

The white only lasted a moment, though, for the acrylic paint of *Homecoming* quickly bled from the canvas to fill the blankness with the desert sunset.

There was the bronze-skinned man, standing at the edge of the cliff. Warrenna stood in his shadow, but she could still make out the red feather in his black hair.

And there was Thomas, standing beside her. And there were his icy blue eyes.

He smiled. "You're here."

Warrenna's eyes felt warm, like a fever. "Why didn't you turn around and say goodbye?"

Where did that come from?

"I didn't want you to see my tears, Mother-to-Doves," Thomas said. "I didn't want you to think I was scared to do what I did. Because I wasn't."

She could understand that. Eyes-of-Dawn-Sky was always so proud. "I wanted to hear your voice one last time," she whispered.

The bronze-skinned man pulled a dagger from the sheath at his waist.

Thomas's face was serene. "I'm sorry."

The man raised the knife, and Thomas placed his hand on Warrenna's shoulder.

"But I knew that we'd see each other again."

The blade swooped toward the man's chest, and Warrenna turned away. But her balance turned with her, and she tumbled to the ground.

When she lifted her head, the sunset and desert were gone, and her bedroom had returned. She sat on the carpet, leaning with the slope of the gradually rotating floor.

Thomas crouched before her, grinning from ear to ear. He offered his hand. "That was interesting, huh?"

She nodded through her dizziness and took his hand. He was warm, but not like the stinging sun. This heat was much softer.

"Is that what happened to you with *Wounded Rider?*" she asked.

"Sort of. It wasn't nearly as cool when I was alone."

She smiled, and lost herself in the warmth and comfort flowing from his eyes. She wanted to stay afloat with him forever, back in that place where time had no meaning, let alone what affliction you were born with. That place where her dirty blood was gone, replaced by chilled champagne sparkling inside her.

"Warrenna!"

Her father's crisp, firm voice. She jumped away from Thomas as though he were covered with spikes.

Richard's goateed face poked in the doorway. "Pack some things. We have to go. Right now."

Suddenly the warmth was gone, replaced by the wet shivering of a walk up a cold beach. *Not again. Not when Thomas could be my cure!*

"Your mother and I need to be in Maldecido right away," Richard continued. "One of our sisters needs our help. We can't leave you here alone. It's not safe."

Warrenna gestured limply to the painting. "But we were just in the painting. I know it sounds strange, but I was *there.*"

"It will only be a couple of days," Richard said. "You can see your friend when you get back."

He turned to Thomas. "I'm sorry son, but you'll have to go. You're welcome here anytime, though. And we'll let you know how those tests turned out."

"Oh. Okay." Thomas picked up his notebook and placed it in Warrenna's hands. "Take this with you. Let me know if any other interesting things happen."

Warrenna was relieved that the trip wasn't going to be permanent, but she still didn't want Thomas to go. They had so much to talk about, and that warm place to visit together. If he left, everything would go back. She would be cursed again, think about blood again, have no future again.

Thomas smiled and touched her cool arm with his warm

hand. "I don't know when I'm going to see you again, but I hope it's soon."

"Same here."

And then, after a polite nod to her father, he was gone.

A couple of minutes later, Warrenna again sat in the dark backseat of the Volvo as the car slowly climbed out of Tebon Canyon. She wondered if Thomas felt as lost as she did just then.

"Mom, do you think Thomas is an angel?"

Alexandria turned around to look at her daughter. "I don't think so, hon." Her dark eyes twinkled with thought. "Because of what we are, angels produce intense fear in us. But I don't think any of us are frightened by your friend." She smiled. "Particularly not you."

Warrenna frowned. "Then what is he?"

"Your aunt Tammy will find out. With Zera's help."

Warrenna toyed with the bandage around her wrist and wondered what Zera had to do with anything. "Did being around him ease your craving?"

Alexandria turned back to face the windshield. "No."

"Are you sure? He wasn't around for you very long."

"Believe me, Renna," Alexandria said quietly. "I am very aware of my craving these days. He didn't affect me in a positive way."

Richard shook his head, answering his daughter's unspoken question.

Warrenna folded her arms. Her parents had to be wrong. Granted, she knew absolutely nothing about angels. But what else could have created that scene in her bedroom? And what else could she call something that could drain away the dull ache of the craving and replace it with the cool, sparkly feeling that coursed through her?

She closed her eyes and pictured the marble beneath her heart. It glowed a brilliant blue, dissolving all the dirt that passed through it.

She fantasized that Thomas could cure her outright. Then she would be like any other sixteen-year-old girl, unbound by things like curses and destiny. She could walk in the sun without fear. She could share absolutely everything with a trusted friend. She could go to a silly dance with a boy.

Smiling, she rested her warm cheek on her shoulder. *Wouldn't that be great? But then, if I became normal, what would Thomas become? Would he have to sacrifice his gift to eliminate my curse?*

She pressed the bandage into her wrist to feel the sting of pain. *I came close to missing out on tonight altogether. Not that I could've known what would happen.*

She stared at the bright desert night above her, at how the stars stayed perfectly still despite the car's acceleration down the quiet highway.

I guess that's the point. How could I possibly know what fate has in store for me?

She jammed her thumb into the bandage and vowed to never give up on fate again.

Chapter 10

The medicine man entered the tent with sorrow in his eyes. He would not look at his patient's face.

"Then it is true," Eyes-of-Dawn-Sky said. "My wound is marked."

Wisdom-of-Elk nodded. "An evil spirit decays you from within, and I cannot draw it out. That is why I have forbidden the tribe from visiting your tent."

Eyes-of-Dawn-Sky rubbed his thigh. It was a deep wound, but he had received far worse in battle before. This little cut was the blow that would end his life?

"Then I am to become a demon?"

"The teachings say you must sacrifice your life on the peak of Zeraphet. It is the only way you can return to the land. You must go alone."

Eyes-of-Dawn-Sky closed his eyes. Zeraphet was four days to the south. He could barely stand on his injured leg, and every breath burned his aching lungs.

He climbed to his feet. "Then I will go."

Wisdom-of-Elk held out a red feather. "Wear this in your hair. It marks you as possessed, and will warn the rest of the tribe."

Eyes-of-Dawn-Sky stuck the feather in his headdress and thanked the old man for his kindness and guidance. But Wisdom-of-Elk would not look at him.

The warrior limped out of his tent. There would be no glorious death in battle for him, but he could at least take the evil spirit inside him far away from his village.

No children played in the dying sunlight as he walked. No women crouched around the fires to talk. No men returned from the hunt. Eyes-of-Dawn-Sky pictured his tribe huddled in their tents, waiting for their doomed brother to leave.

But one woman stood by her tent, out of the shadows, erect, facing him. Mother-to-Doves did not flinch at the red feather in his hair.

He walked by her without saying a word. He could not let her see him suffer.

He could not bear to see her ashamed.

Thomas woke slowly, without any doubt of whom or where he was. Bright sunlight shone onto the foot of his bed, and he pulled his feet out from under the covers to wiggle his toes in the warmth.

He wondered how Warrenna, wherever she was, saw that same light. Probably as something to hide from, something to avoid at all costs. She probably felt that way all her life.

He smiled and rubbed his eyes. *Soon she'll see the sun in a much different way. The way I have all* my *life.*

He stretched his shoulders and yawned. Why was Warrenna so worried about what happened to him as he cured her curse? The warm glow inside him more than made up for any sorrow he felt when they were together.

Thomas waved his fingers in and out of the yellow rays and watched the shadows flicker on the sheets. He wondered what his dreams had to do with all of this. Maybe they were a side effect of being an angel amongst humans.

"The Angel Thomas," he whispered, and smiled. "That might explain a few things."

He climbed out of bed and sat at his desk to record his dream. He opened the journal and took the cap off his pen, but didn't start writing. Something felt wrong.

And then he knew. His alarm hadn't gone off.

"Oh, crap, the game!"

Coach wanted him at the gym by 9:30. He checked the clock. 9:22.

He groaned and grabbed his clothes. *God, out-of-it all week, and now I'm going to be late for the actual game!*

As he stripped off his pajamas in preparation for the world's fastest shower, Thomas remembered that he still hadn't recorded last night's dream yet.

He dove into the lukewarm water anyway. "Medicine Man," he said, trying to hold the image of the old man in his mind. "Medicine Man, Medicine Man."

As he drove, he thought about scribbling down some notes about the dream, but then shook his head. *It'd be pretty stupid of me to wreck my car because I was trying to write. Stupid, like forgetting to set my freaking alarm.*

She opened the door, and there was Tommy, with his bright eyes and his steady smile.

A gust of cold air blew in. She would need a jacket this morning, just like everyone else.

Tommy led her out of the dark room, to the outside. He held

a big black umbrella in his left hand and he shared the shelter with her.

He wasn't shielding her from the sun, but from the sprinkles of rain. She didn't need protection from the sun anymore.

She wrapped her arm around his side, under his coat, to feel his wonderful warmth. He put his hand on her shoulder, drawing her closer, and together they ventured into the parking lot.

Warrenna didn't know where they were going, but it didn't matter.

We can go anywhere, we can do anything, as long as we're together....

Warrenna rolled over and squeezed her sides. The marble inside her glowed a faint blue, shooting bubbly warmth into her heart.

Eventually the fantasy subsided, and she wondered where she was. The room was dark, but she could make out a few details: a sliding closet door, a wooden chair, a trunk next to the chair, a closed door she assumed was the exit.

A lamp with three bulbs on a pole stood near the bed. The lowest light didn't work, but the middle one turned on for her.

The walls were bleak and dirty, the brownish carpet thin and fringed. Two things set her mind at ease, though. First, her shoulder bag sat in the closet. Second, a thick black blanket hung tacked to one of the walls, almost certainly concealing a window. Wherever she was, the place was friendly to her kind.

Warrenna rubbed her forehead as she tried to remember the previous night. She remembered drifting in and out of sleep as she thought about that warm cliff with the stunning sunset. She also thought about Thomas, smiling beside her, holding her hand.

She remembered endless driving, switching vehicles at least once, and her father giving passwords to wary-eyed people in empty parking lots.

Probably didn't miss much. Just more stuff I can't do anything about.

She wondered how long she'd been asleep, but the room had no clock. Yesterday's clothes still clung to her body, and her hair felt greasy. Wherever she was, she needed a shower.

She rolled out of bed, grabbed her bag from the closet and opened the door. A room full of light greeted her: bright sunlight, scraping away her skin, burrowing into her corneas. Instinctively her hand went up to shield her eyes.

"Oh, you're up. Let me get that for you."

The voice was familiar, and through her fingers, Warrenna saw Uncle Vince drawing some heavy blue curtains in front of a sliding glass door. The painful light was quickly extinguished.

He wiped his hands on his faded blue jeans. "Good morning, sleepyhead. It's nearly one. I was about to make sure you were still breathing."

Warrenna shrugged and yawned. She could see the rest of the room now. More dingy carpet, an overstuffed blue sofa with tears in the fabric, a coffee table with a cracked glass surface, an ancient television with knobs to change the channel.

"Where are we?" she asked. "Where are my mom and dad?"

Uncle Vince leaned his wiry frame against one of the blank walls. "This is the apartment your father and I shared in college. We keep it for occasions like this. That bed you slept on? That's actually the same bed we had back then. It probably felt like it, yeah?"

She returned his smile, and he continued. "Rick would sleep on it during the afternoon, work his graveyards at that crappy all-night taco stand, then go to class right after work. Those were the days. I don't know how he kept it up. I hardly ever saw him."

"That's nice, Uncle Vince. But where are my mom and dad?"

He touched his forehead. "Yeah, right, your parents. They're over with the Orphans, trying to help a friend of ours. They figured you probably didn't want to hang out over there. Plus you were passed out. I've never seen anybody sleep that hard."

Warrenna sighed. The Orphans were the group that her parents founded, vampires determined to stay human, and fanatical about Zera. When she was small, she knew them only as friends of her parents. But even before she knew who they really were, she got a strange feeling whenever she was around any of them. Their eyes always held a preternatural clearness and intensity when looking at Warrenna, like they were trying to remember every move she made so they could run home and record it all in their diaries. Her parents and Aunt Tammy seemed to be the only Orphans that treated Warrenna like a person and not some celebrity.

"It was nice of them to spare me," she told Uncle Vince. "What's going on?"

"This friend of ours—her name is Necole—she's right on the edge. Your folks are gonna go all-out to bring her back. Necole's been with us since damn near the beginning. We were just starting to hunt other vampires, and Necole was a vital part of the team."

His eyes drifted upward, focusing on a spot about a foot over her head. "Those were the days. We'd meet in this little room, planning raids on vampire nests. There was your mom and your dad, Tamara and me, Luis, Necole, and Stefan. Man, Stefan was still with us back then. Those were the days."

Warrenna sighed in exasperation. "What do you mean, Necole's on the edge? Is she going to kill herself?"

Uncle Vince bowed his bald head. "No, it's, uh, that vampire thing. You know. Something awful happened to her, and Tamara had to put Necole in a coma to keep her from, you know, going all the way." He swallowed. "Don't tell your parents I told you."

Her response was a shrug. *It's just a matter of time for each of us. Except for me, maybe.*

She noticed that the bandage on her wrist was gone. Two

ugly white scars were all that remained of her ordeal in the bathtub. Had the Last Resort done the trick? Or was Tommy responsible?

Even though she knew the answer, she asked, "What happens if they can't bring Necole back?"

Vince shook his head. "We can't just let vampires run around killing people and spreading the curse. If she turns, we'll have to end her suffering."

Warrenna remembered her mother's uneasy steps, and the new black cane. How long did she have until something happened to her? Who would be the one to end her mother's suffering?

She swallowed hard. "How come you hang around us vampires, Uncle V? All we are is struggle and loss."

Uncle Vince folded his skinny arms. "I've never heard it put quite that way, dear. Your father and I were friends in Bascomville long before that vampire attacked him. I'm not one to let a little thing like craving human blood come between me and my buddies."

Warrenna knew her uncle was trying to cheer her up, but she didn't feel like letting him. "But don't you get worried? One day, one of us might lose control and go after all that life flowing through your veins."

He shook his head again. "Nah, I know you wouldn't. Plus, thanks to Tamara, er, your aunt Tammy, I know more about you guys than most vampires do. I've got some ways to defend myself if one of you slips over the edge." His eyes brightened. "But hey, that's not in your future anymore, huh? What with Major Tom and all."

Warrenna smiled at Uncle Vince's nickname for Tommy. "Yeah, maybe not. Did you find out anything from Thomas's sample?"

She pictured Tommy's blood rolling around in a test tube, sticking to the sides. Then she imagined a dark line of crimson sliding down his bare, tanned chest. The line flowed down his sternum, followed a rib, and drew a half-circle around a pectoral.

The bitter, coppery smell filled her nostrils. The marble pulsed black, and when she dared to think about his taste, crimson drenched the room.

Release me! We must have his blood! It will fuel us for decades!

Warrenna shook her head at the voice inside her. *No,* she told it. *He's not even here.*

Then she gasped. *Er, I mean, no. I could never hurt Tommy! He might be the cure.*

"He just seems really healthy," Uncle Vince was saying. He smiled. "I bet you think about him a lot."

Warrenna blushed and tried her hardest to control her breathing. The crimson faded away, and the marble swirled black and orange.

Whoa. And that was just from thinking *about his blood.*

Uncle Vince hadn't noticed anything. He was still smiling at her.

"Uh, so," Warrenna said, "you, um, don't think he's an angel?"

Uncle Vince's drifting gaze went still for a moment, like he noticed something far away. "No, I don't think so. It might sound hard to believe, but I've seen some angels in my time, Renny-Penny. Honest-to-goodness, beings-of-light-and-peace *angels*. Been in the same room with one. They make you feel so comfortable, like you're home, after a long, long journey, and you wish they'd never leave so you could always feel that way."

He trailed off to a whisper, and his gaunt face turned melancholy for a moment. But then his gaze began wandering again. "That's a story for another time. Your Thomas is no angel. I'm sure. Positive. Confident."

Warrenna frowned. "Then what is he?"

Uncle Vince grinned again. "Something else."

She rolled her eyes. *Yeah, some new type of angel you and my parents have never seen before.*

"You wanna see him?"

Warrenna thought he was kidding, but Uncle Vince's face

was serious. "What? Now? Wouldn't my parents get mad if I suddenly left town?"

"We won't go anywhere, and neither will Major Tom. But you'll be with him. He won't know it, but you'll practically see through his eyes."

"What do you mean? How?"

"Look, Tamara asked me to investigate any psychic link between you and Thomas while she helps out Necole. I'm betting that whatever you two have going between you is strong enough that I can ride it all the way to wherever he is. Bascomville, Maldecido, Timbuktu, wherever."

Warrenna swallowed hard and followed Uncle Vince's floating gaze around the room. "I didn't, uh, know you were psychic, Uncle V."

He laughed. "I'm not psychic, silly. You are. Or at least your vampire form is."

"I am? Er, it is?"

He nodded. "Vampires have powerful minds, capable of operating on levels that we humans can barely comprehend. Obviously all that power is drenched in evil, so it remains unavailable to anyone wishing to retain his or her humanity. But the potential is there. And over the years, I've learned how to tap into it from the outside."

Warrenna rubbed her eyes. Even if it was the afternoon, it was still too early to think this hard. "So you're saying that you can use my brainpower, but I can't?"

"Well, you can use that power, but only in your other form. And I have *no* desire to meet Evil Renny."

Yeah, she's pretty scary.

"How did you learn this stuff, Uncle V? Did you go to some kind of weirdo academy? I bet you got straight A's in the *messing with the occult* classes."

Uncle Vince snorted, and his eyes twitched back and forth. Warrenna couldn't decide if he was annoyed or fighting laughter.

"I've been looking for a cure for the curse for a long time, Renny. And not every source of supernatural knowledge is as mum as Zera, or as untrusting as the angels. Some of them are a little more interested in power." He shook his head. "But that's not important right now. Do you want to be with Major Tom or not?"

She smiled. "Sure I do. I'd like to see how he's handling all this. For his sake, of course." *Even if he isn't bleeding.* Warrenna bit her tongue. *I have to stop thinking about Tommy's blood.*

"Of course." Uncle Vince tried to wink, but the resulting twitch looked more like a facial tic. He gestured to a hallway on her right. "Take your shower. I'll get ready."

"Okay." She tapped the side of her head. "Anything I need to do up here?"

"Nope, the work is on my end." He disappeared around a corner, into a tiny kitchen. "If you have something of his," he called, "it would make it easier for me."

She fished Thomas's dream-journal from her bag and placed it on a counter. "Will this help?"

Uncle Vince's shifting eyes locked onto the cover of the book, and he held his position for several seconds. "Yes," he eventually said. "Yes, this should help a lot."

"Okay."

Warrenna slowly backed away and wondered what his intense eyes really saw.

Then she decided she didn't want to know.

Which is creepier: the tainted potential in my head, or that Uncle Vince is about to use it?

The hot water felt terrific on her kinked-up back, but she hurried through her bathing anyway. If she reached that sparkly feeling again, it wouldn't really matter how creepy the process was.

The living room was darker and cooler when she returned, and Warrenna wished she had spent more time drying her hair; the dampness of it made her shiver. Uncle Vince sat cross-legged in the center of the carpet with his eyes closed. Squat white candles stood in chipped saucers on three sides of him, forming a triangle.

"Are you ready?" he asked without opening his eyes.

"I guess."

"Good. Light the candles for me."

Some matches lay in one of the saucers, and Warrenna carefully lit each of the candles. She noticed Thomas's open journal resting just in front of Uncle Vince's still body.

"Now sit in front of me," he said. "This is going to be a little disorienting, but keep in mind that you're completely safe here. It will only be a matter of moments before you're back in your own body."

Warrenna stopped halfway into her crouch. "Wait. I'm going to leave my body?"

Uncle Vince smiled patiently. "No, but it will feel like it, and that naturally produces a bit of panic. Again, you're safe. You'll be back very soon."

"Um, okay."

"If you're frightened, you don't have to come. But I *do* need you inside the triangle."

Warrenna shook her head and sat, crossing her legs like Uncle Vince's. "I'll come with. I want to see how he is."

"Good show. You have your father's courage."

His hands lifted from his knees and opened to her in one graceful motion. "Take my hands, and look unblinking into my eyes."

His palms were warm, but the feeling was thinner, hollower than Tommy's warmth.

She thought about Thomas, his eyes, how clear they looked

when they were inside *Homecoming* together, and how that clearness was reflected in the marble beneath her heart. Her blood tingled in response. *Get ready, curse. You're about to get even weaker.*

Uncle Vince's eyelids parted, and two brilliant pools of blue swirled where his eyes should have been. The holes in his head looked like tiny televisions glowing with blue static.

White light filled the room, and Warrenna's body went limp. *Safe, back very soon.*

Thomas blinked and rubbed his eyes. His vision went bluish for a moment, like when he stepped into the shade of the house after pulling weeds in the bright sun.

Then he saw Coach Reeves standing before him, wearing an incredulous look on his face.

"Uh, you can count on me, Coach. I'm ready to go."

"Yeah, you better be," Coach Reeves mumbled. "Look, son, just don't turn the ball over. Give me three good minutes till we can get Diaz back in there."

"Yes, sir."

Ten minutes remained in the game, and Chiricahua was up by only six. Sunnyslope was giving the Coyotes a better game than Thomas expected. One thing had gone how Thomas expected, though. He hadn't played a single minute. Coach only needed him now because Diaz, the starter, was in foul trouble, and Hansen, the backup, had just twisted his ankle.

Thomas walked onto the court feeling strange, and it wasn't just the chilly feeling in his legs that he always got when he entered a game for the first time. He couldn't put his finger on it, but something felt different.

He took the in-bounds pass and dribbled up the court. Coach

held up his fist. That meant he should get the ball to Brendan and let the play start with him.

Thomas fired a crisp bounce pass to his friend, who stood near the baseline with his back to the basket. Thomas then sprinted to the corner on the opposite side of the court. If the play went like he thought, he would be open. Sunnyslope would double-team Brendan, and let the ball come around to Thomas to take the open shot.

The ball came to him. He caught it cleanly, got a good grip, brought it to his chin.

It won't go in.

Thomas knew it like he knew the times-tables. The shot was too difficult.

So instead of shooting, he calmly dribbled toward the basket. Defenders came to meet him, so he stopped and looked for someone to pass to.

That's when Thomas realized why he was feeling strange. It was because he could see *everything*.

He saw all of the players on the court and where they stood in relation to each other. He saw the cheerleaders, the referees, the coaches. Everyone was clear and in-focus. He could even see Mariah in the crowd. Her golden hair was swept away from her face, like she just walked out of a salon.

Thomas blinked. *I probably ought to get rid of the ball.*

Owes was open under the basket. Thomas took one step toward out-of-bounds and threw the ball at him.

The pass surprised him, but Owes managed to catch the ball and get up a shot. He missed, but the whistle blew for a foul.

Thomas wandered out to his position at half-court and idly watched the lanky center take his free throws. Thomas had been tuned in to a game before. He had moved well, remembered the plays, kept his feet moving and so on. But never anything like this. He could feel what was going to happen, could sense how he could change events to work to his benefit.

He took a deep breath. The air was clean and invigorating, and carried a whiff of something familiar, something spicy.

Ginger. Like in Warrenna's room last night.

He backed into his defensive stance. *Maybe that's it. I know I'm healing Warrenna, so now I can see all this. I can be all this!*

A rebound bounced off the rim right into his hands. He passed the ball upcourt and jogged after it, wondering why Warrenna wasn't more excited about whatever was happening to them.

The ball swung back to him as he stood near the top of the painted area. For a moment he just watched the players move. Then he drove to the left side of the basket, jumped up, twisted his body and flung the ball behind his back.

The ball flew across the court and hit Corwyn in the chest. The Sunnyslope players were so stunned that Corwyn had plenty of time to collect himself and launch a three-point shot.

Thomas jogged back to play defense as the shot went *swish,* like he knew it would. He stopped at half-court and gave afterthought high-fives to his teammates as they passed.

Maybe Warrenna isn't used to good things happening to her. Maybe after she's cured some more, she'll see how wonderful this is.

He took a step to his left, which allowed him to steal a pass, and dribbled down the court at less-than-top speed so a defender could get between him and the basket just as he approached the goal.

He winked at Brendan, who trailed the play behind him.

What could be bad about feeling like this?

Thomas used his allotted two steps to turn all the way around and bend over, placing his body directly beneath the basket and shoving the Sunnyslope player nearly out-of-bounds with his backside. He used the momentum to slam the ball into the floor, bouncing it high into the air. Brendan jumped up, grabbed the ball and slammed it into the hoop in one powerful motion.

The crowd exploded in cheers.

Brendan's face was radiant with astonished delight. "Oh my GOD, what a pass!"

Thomas could barely hear him over the jubilation of the crowd. He smiled and playfully shoved his teammate.

Sunnyslope called time-out, so Thomas jogged to the bench. Each of his teammates wanted a high-five, and most of them slapped his back.

"Jesus Christ, son!" Coach Reeves yelled over the cheering crowd. "What the hell's gotten into you?"

Thomas shrugged. "Just one of those days, sir!"

Reeves shook his head. "Enjoy it while it lasts, son!"

The pulsing blue cloud shifted and swirled above the barren, dusty earth. But it was also shrinking, evaporating.

Eventually Warrenna realized that the earth was actually the dirty carpet, and the cloud was all that remained of the blue static. The spot drifted across her vision like a sun-tracer.

She could still hear the roar of the crowd. The din faded slowly, at about the rate the blue cloud dissipated. The sensation reminded her of something, but she couldn't put her finger on what.

But that didn't matter, because that sparkly feeling again surged through her chest and into her neck. And the marble was back to a serene blue.

Warrenna smiled. *Doesn't look like he's suffering, that's for sure.*

She lifted her head from the floor and found Uncle Vince still sitting cross-legged in the triangle of extinguished candles.

He rubbed his eyes. "You're back?"

"I think so. I had no idea he was such a good player."

"He isn't. You were affecting him. How do you feel?"

Then she remembered. The blue cloud dissipating reminded her of slowly waking from a pleasant dream. She couldn't remember that last time that had happened.

Wait a second, did he say *affecting?* "What was that, Uncle V?"

"I said, how do you feel?"

"I'm fine. Just a little dizzy. But what was that about me affecting him?"

Uncle Vince's eyes were back to their shifting. His gaze now centered on her shoulder. "It was pretty evident that he could feel your presence. And given your link, I don't think it's coincidence that he was playing out of his head."

"So what does that mean?"

"I don't know. I saw something strange in there." Uncle Vince's voice was low, almost foreboding. But then he cleared his throat and looked away. "But I need to meet with Tamara before I say anything else."

She touched his knee. "Come on, Uncle V. I can take it. What did you see?"

"Uh-uh. No way. I might be wrong, and it would just worry you for no reason."

Warrenna frowned. She had no idea if Uncle Vince was telling the truth or not, but it was obvious she wasn't going to get anything more out of him. So instead, she asked, "What *are* you sure of, Uncle Vince?"

He looked back to her, or at least to her left ear. "I'll tell you this much, Renny. I wouldn't be surprised if Zera was behind this whole situation."

Chapter II

Thomas carefully watched the reflection in his bathroom mirror as he ran the comb through his wet hair. He wondered how Warrenna groomed herself if she couldn't see her own face in a mirror. Did all vampires have their hair brushed by other vampires?

That brought to mind a field of baboons picking bugs out of each other's fur. The vampires would then be like bloodsucking baboons.

That's silly. That reflection-thing must be another myth.

The baboons reminded him of a dream in which he could see a savannah stretching for miles in each direction, like he stood atop a mountain in Africa. The feeling was similar to the one he experienced on the basketball court earlier in the afternoon.

Jane Ferrick's party was still an hour away, so he had plenty of time to browse his shelf of dreams before he had to pick up Mariah.

How long ago did he dream about the African savannah? Six months? Nine months?

He picked out a journal from last summer, near his birthday, and flipped a few pages. He knew the odds of finding the right entry were terrible, but he liked the snapshot flash that always accompanied scanning any page in his journal. Then all he had to do was close his eyes, and a few moments of the dream would play out again for him. It was like remembering adventures with old friends.

A note in his mother's handwriting was folded between two of the pages. It began, *To Tommy, on his 17th birthday.*

The letter was filled with heartwarming messages of pride and hope for the future, and Thomas rolled his eyes at how corny his mother could get. But the bottom of the page caught his attention:

Always remember that with God, anything is possible. A boy like you, born six weeks premature, can grow up to be strong and healthy. A mother like me can emerge from a car accident convinced that her son had died before he could be born. But God proved me wrong.

That is why we named you Thomas. Because, like the apostle doubted that Jesus had risen on the third day, on that hospital bed I doubted that God had kept you here with us. I thank Him every day that He did.

Always remember that miracles happen, Tommy. You're one of them.

The note fell from Thomas's hands. He didn't think much about his mother's words back then, but that was before he met Warrenna.

What if the real Thomas Gelbaugh was never born, and the being that stood in front of this bookcase took his place?

He bit into both cheeks. *But how do I tell if that's true? I can't exactly send a urine sample to a laboratory to see if I come up positive for angel.*

He closed the journal and shoved it back into its spot on the shelf. Mariah was expecting him.

He wondered how he could have a good time at the party with his head full of dreams and angels.

And then he wondered if angels were even allowed to have a good time.

Leg hurts with every step. Water won't last the night. Must keep moving. Breathing hurts. So far to go. Rest. Breath won't come. No shade to stop beneath.

Movement in distance. Eyes hazy. It moves in a line, like a person. I take feather from hair, wave. They can't come near me. Person keeps walking, coming toward me.

STAY AWAY! My yell brings coughs. Must go, can't stop cough, get away from person, GO! Leg hurts, must keep moving, take the spirit away from everyone, so far to go...

Warrenna took a bite of her muffin and shook her head, careful to keep the crumbs from landing on Thomas's journal. No great inspiration to sketch anything had come to her, but with this latest entry, she decided to move her pencil around on her sketchbook and see if anything happened on its own.

She scribbled a bit and took another bite. The muffin was particularly delicious. She supposed the blueberries were fresh. She put her pencil down and went to see if Uncle Vince had eaten the rest of the half-dozen.

When she reached the living room, Warrenna was surprised to find the drapes open to a dusky orange sky. Was it sunset already?

Uncle Vince sat cross-legged on the sofa with his eyes closed. "Your parents are on their way," he said without turning to her. "They'll be happy to see how much you've eaten."

Both statements confused her. First, how did he know her parents were coming? She never heard any phone ring. Second, eating one muffin was hardly cause for celebration, even among the most cursed of their kind.

"I don't get it."

"You really lost yourself in the book." Uncle Vince fixed his deep blue eyes on her. "Your parents called about a half-hour ago, and I've replaced the muffin before you five times. You never noticed me, did you?"

Warrenna pursed her lips. "Uh, no, I guess I didn't. You're not pulling my leg, are you?"

Uncle Vince shook his head. "That was quite a journey you went on this morning. It took a lot out of you, and that book was just what you needed to recharge. It even made you crave regular food."

He was right. She was still hungry. She closed her eyes and found the marble shining blue, sending warm waves of light through her chest.

"Wow," she breathed. "The journal did this to me?"

Uncle Vince grinned. "That book glows, Renny. And I'll bet it affects you more than anybody else on this planet."

Warrenna smirked. *Still think he's not an angel?*

She opened her mouth to ask Uncle Vince as much, but just then, the outside door banged open. Warrenna's parents stood in the doorway. Alexandria had one arm around Richard's neck as he half-supported her weight.

Warrenna quickly moved to help her, but her mother waved her off. "I'm fine, Renna," Alexandria said in a raspy voice. "I just need to sit down for a moment." She shuffled across the thin carpet to the couch. "How are you feeling?"

"I feel good," Warrenna said. "I ate a bunch of muffins."

Alexandria smiled weakly. "That's good to hear."

Richard closed the outside door and leaned against it. Warrenna couldn't help but notice his slumped shoulders.

"Dad, how's Necole?"

Richard raised an eyebrow toward Uncle Vince, who

shrugged. "She wanted to know where you were. What was I going to do, lie?"

"It's okay, Vincent," Alexandria said. "You saved us some time." She turned to Warrenna. "Despite all of our efforts, Necole is still lost in her coma. I know you don't like being around the Orphans, but I was hoping that you would go back with us. We could use your help."

"Me? What help would I be?"

Alexandria cleared her throat. "All day, we performed our cleansing ritual with as many of Zera's followers as we could muster. And all day, we've seen no response from Necole."

"Someone," Richard said, "made her bleed for a very long time."

"Someone or some thing made her bleed," Alexandria corrected. "We don't know what it was that drained her for so long. Her attacker must have known that catastrophic blood loss can make one of us turn. But it's not like a vampire to run from us."

She turned back to Warrenna. "Regardless, I think your presence would make the ritual more powerful. You are as much a child of Zera's as you are of mine."

Warrenna folded her arms. *Just like Mother to guilt-trip me into worshiping Zera.*

Richard read Warrenna's frown. "We're not asking you to become a follower this instant. But your mother's right. You're bound to affect the ritual, and right now we're running out of options."

Warrenna swallowed hard. How many Orphans would ask how she was feeling, or if she needed anything, or if there was anything they could do for her? *Ugh!*

She looked to her mother's drawn face. *But what if Mom was the one in need of help?*

She sighed. It wasn't that much to ask. Besides, what else was she going to do tonight?

"Okay, I'll do it. When do we go?"

"As soon as you're ready," Alexandria replied.

Uncle Vince nodded. "Good. I need to see Tamara as soon as possible."

"Hey man, great moves out there today."

Thomas gave the boy a smile and mumbled some thanks, then re-buried his gaze in the punch bowl. The red liquid carried the telltale kick of one of Corwyn's spikings, but he filled up his glass anyway.

He took a swig of the bitter brew. His eyes met Brendan's in the crowd of students dancing in Jane Ferrick's living room, and his friend grinned at him. Brendan yelled something, but Thomas couldn't hear over the thumping music. He raised his glass in salute anyway. Brendan nodded and turned back into the strobe light.

"The girl's a vampire," Thomas mumbled into the music. "But she's fighting it, and I'm somehow curing her. Maybe because I'm really an angel in a human body. Don't tell anyone, okay?"

He took a long pull from his drink. *The more fun the party gets, the more irrelevant it feels.*

He made his way around the punch table to find the bathroom again. But as he shouldered his way through the partiers he saw Mariah dancing in the next room.

She moved easily, happily, but with a reserved smile that reminded Thomas of someone crawling into a comfortable bed after a long day of work. A white dress hugged her curves, but not immodestly. *What about Mariah?*

Her eyes found his. She smiled broadly and moved to him, her golden curls bouncing with each step.

She touched his shoulder and shouted over the music, "You should be happier!"

Thomas tacked on a smile. "Yeah, I know."

Mariah put a finger in the air, then took a step into the kitchen. After a moment, she emerged with a confused, shirtless Owes.

"Brian," she yelled, "what are you doing after high school?"

"Dude," Owes replied, "I got no idea. I guess I'll get a job or something."

"Yeah? Does not knowing bother you?"

"Nah. I just know I won't have to go to school anymore."

Mariah smiled again. "Thanks, Brian. You can go now!"

"Whatever, crazy Chiquita!" He disappeared back into the kitchen.

Thomas shook his head. He appreciated what Mariah was trying, but he couldn't pretend that Owes's oblivion made him feel any better. "I wish it was that simple."

She frowned at him, then grabbed his wrist and pulled him through the kitchen, out a sliding glass door and onto the vacant back porch. Low floodlights shone onto the swimming pool, giving the water an eerie blue glow.

Mariah closed the door behind them, cutting the music's volume in half, and rubbed her bare arms to keep warm. "C'mon, Tom. You probably haven't noticed, but the best party in history is happening in there. Enjoy this moment while it's here."

"I know, I'm sorry. But it all feels, you know, irrelevant." Thomas stopped himself. The jungle juice was loosening his tongue, but he had to make sure Warrenna's secret didn't slip.

Mariah looked at her feet for a moment. Her voice was quiet. "I think I know what this is about. Can you do something for me?"

He shrugged his shoulders. "Sure."

"Follow me inside. It's too cold out here to talk."

She grasped his sweaty hand and led him through the door. They snaked their way through the poker game in the kitchen, through the dark den's kung-fu movie, and up some hardwood stairs.

Mariah opened a door and flipped a light switch. "This is Jane's sister's room," she whispered. "She moved out a long time ago."

The room was decorated sparsely. A bed with a burgundy comforter, a dark wood chest of drawers, and a wooden rocking chair were the only furniture Thomas saw. Mariah sat on the bed and gestured for Thomas to do the same. The music thumped through his feet, but otherwise the room was still.

"Listen," Mariah said, "you know what my earliest memory of you is? It's on the playground in elementary school. I can still see you yelling at Matt McDougal to get off the swing because 'Muh-wiah didn't get a tuhn.' And you know what? That's the way it's always been with you. I didn't realize it until recently, but you have always thought of everyone else first."

"Not always."

"Name once."

"Well, I've been kind of self-absorbed all night."

"That may be. But do you know why?"

I've got a pretty good idea. Before he could respond, Mariah continued.

"It's because all this talk about the future, and college, and what we're going to do with ourselves has forced you to think about yourself. And you hesitate, because it doesn't feel right. But I think you're going to keep feeling overwhelmed and swept away by life until you take a good hard look at yourself and find out what it is you really want."

Thomas sighed. *There's also the angel question running through my head. That might make me feel a bit overwhelmed. But I can't tell you that, can I?*

"I'll make it a little easier for you," Mariah continued. "Let me tell you what I want. I want to go to SAU and experience life out on my own, get an education, and have some fun without going totally nuts. I want to take on this new stage of life, and I want to do that with you."

She took his hand in hers. "I want you to be by my side as we do all these new things in that new place," she said. "And do you know why?"

Thomas shook his head.

Her smile returned, and suddenly her eyes softened and began to shine. "Because I love you, Thomas. And there's nobody I'd rather plunge into the unknown with than you."

Thomas's heart slowly thudded as he stared, disbelieving, at the tear slipping down Mariah's perfect cheek. Did she really just say that she loved him?

"Okay, Thomas," she said. "Now you have to tell me what you want. I have to know, right now."

Thomas basked in Mariah's easy smile. *Have I ever wanted anyone else to say those words to me?*

And then he moved his hand behind her neck and drew her into a long, deep kiss. She pulled him closer, and his blood ignited as he filled his lungs with her sweet scent.

They fell onto the bed and she climbed on top of him, holding the kiss as her body rested on his.

And then, through the haze of hormone and heat, Thomas saw a pair of sad gray eyes. The sorrow tumbled down on him like an avalanche, heavy and inevitable. The scent of ground black pepper stung his nose and eyes.

Mariah can't love me. She doesn't know who I really am.

"No."

Mariah cocked her head. "No?"

"It's not right."

"Sure it is." Her breath was warm on his neck. "I haven't had that much to drink. This is all me here. This is what I want. This is who I want. Or whom. Whatever." She giggled.

"No." Thomas's hands knuckled his burning eyes. "You don't understand. You're beautiful, and the only one I've ever really wanted, but it's not right."

She finally slid off him, chin quivering. "Why not? What's wrong?"

The air was thick with pepper. When his hands moved from his eyes, tears spilled down his cheeks.

"I can't. I don't think I'm human."

Mariah called his name as he fled the room, but Thomas didn't look back. He stumbled down the stairs, turned his ankle, banged his knee into something. He ran, but the sadness stayed with him, like a film covering every sticky inch of skin, or a poisoned gas polluting every breath he took. He felt like he'd robbed a hundred struggling families or broken a hundred promises to his mother.

It was when he fell into the driver's seat of his car that the strangeness of his behavior finally dawned on him. A dream scenario with Mariah just played out for him, but he ran from her like she was the creature of the night!

Shivers ran up his sides. *Why did I run away? Why did I think it was so wrong?*

He couldn't remember. Or maybe he never knew.

He pressed his forehead into the icy steering wheel.

"What's happening to me?"

Chapter 12

Thomas held his breath as he crossed the threshold into St. Stephen's, and then blew it out when he realized he felt no different.

He slowly dipped his finger into the font of holy water on the wall. Exactly the same slickness he remembered. He let the water touch his forehead as he made the sign of the cross. Nothing special happened.

The oaken bas-reliefs depicting the Stations of the Cross hung quietly on the walls. The statue of the Virgin Mary gazed emptily from beneath her midnight-blue habit.

Thomas frowned and followed his parents down an aisle. St. Stephen's had no pews. Instead, rows of padded chairs were carefully arranged in two sections, one left, one right. He couldn't remember ever missing a Sunday service.

Thomas massaged his aching temple and took a seat beside his father. He had half-expected the holy water to glow, or the crucifix to radiate a cool breeze that only he could feel. But everything about the church felt exactly the same as last week.

If I were an angel, wouldn't all this holy stuff feel different? Like it was better?

The left side of Thomas's face thumped painfully as the familiar ceremony moved along. He tried saying the prayers and responses more earnestly then ever before, but nothing happened. Eventually he concluded that if he were going to feel anything different, the time would come at communion. He supposed the body and blood of Christ might react to the divinity inside him now that he was aware of it.

Thinking about blood made him wonder how Warrenna would feel in a place like St. Stephen's. Would she be frightened, angry or impassive? Would the holy water burn her skin like in the movies? Would she cower from the crucifix like it was a loaded gun?

Would those weary gray eyes flash red?

Thomas winced as he recalled the party, how he ran away from Mariah after seeing those same eyes. But what were Warrenna's eyes doing in his head? Why did they come up at the worst possible time?

Replaying last night's events passed the time, but Thomas focused on the present when he noticed the man walking to the podium to deliver the homily. He wore the same white suit Thomas had seen in the art hallway at Chiricahua High. He glanced at the song list: "Today's homily given by guest speaker Derek O'Neal."

The man cleared his throat, nodded at the priest, then looked across the congregation with small blue eyes. "Good morning. I come to you today, brothers and sisters, to talk about our young people. As you know, too many turn away from the Church when they reach their volatile years. Their rudderless souls make our young people lonely, and they become easy prey for the wolves that feed on stray lambs."

Just for an instant, so fast that Thomas didn't think anyone else saw, the man looked at him, then back to the congregation before continuing.

"I can think of no better example of this than a poor soul I encountered a few years ago in Maldecido. His name was Jimmy, and he came to Southern Arizona University from a tiny town in Indiana. He was drawn by the sunny climate, the pretty girls, and the promise of something bright and different.

"Now, Jimmy was a little naïve. And he was lonely, being so far away from home. But he found some people that seemed friendly. They also seemed to share his devout Christian beliefs, and that was comforting to him. But Jimmy didn't know that he'd fallen in with a cult.

"This particular cult laced their refreshments with powerful hallucinogens, and from his journals I know that Jimmy had false, miraculous-seeming visions. He thought he could heal the wounded simply by thinking about them. He claimed he could visit other worlds, speak to humans on other planets in the form of an angel, spreading the Lord's word to millions and millions of what he called 'other souls.'"

Thomas's eyeballs turned to ice. *Angel?*

"Jimmy became obsessed with this mission of his. He dropped out of school and cut off all contact with his family back in Indiana. Three months later, some hikers found his emaciated body in the desert. Jimmy was dead. He was only eighteen."

O'Neal pounded the podium with his fist. "We must work harder to keep our youth in the Christian community! Our young people are so desperate to feel special, to feel part of something, that they buy fully into the deceptions handed them by frauds. Too many young people have been programmed to fulfill the desires of the demons in Maldecido, Phoenix, and Los Angeles."

Scattered murmurings greeted his words. Some of the group looked confused; others nodded as though they agreed. All turned rapt attention on him as he said, "Take the time to show your sons and daughters that they are loved, that they are children of God, even if they think that's *uncool*. When they are lured by a cult, they will be armed with the love of their community and of their God, and they will easily repel any charlatan's advances."

O'Neal's tiny eyes fixed on Thomas. "And if you think

Bascomville's small size protects it from evil, know that I have seen evidence of that very same cult in the halls of your own Chiricahua High School."

There were gasps from the congregation now, and Thomas's blood ran cold. Could a drug be responsible for that episode with the painting in the hallway? Could it have caused the missing time on Wednesday?

"So communicate with your children," O'Neal finished. "Love them, and bring them to worship. Let the light of our Lord keep away the servants of darkness."

What O'Neal was saying didn't make sense. Warrenna originally told him to stay away, and neither she nor her family had asked for anything from him. They seemed to be nothing like the cult O'Neal was talking about. But they certainly made him feel special.

Thomas gnawed on his cheek. *Feeling all glowy inside makes all of this vampire stuff feel natural.* But where were those feelings now? Where were they last night? Could they have come from a drug, one that was wearing off?

O'Neal sat, communion began, and Thomas took his wafer and sip of wine. The sacrament felt exactly the same as every other time he went through the motions. He returned to his seat and stared at his shoes. The mass was nearly over and he had no answers, no special feelings he could use to figure out what he was. Just more questions.

Warrenna woke with a gasp, recoiling from whatever it was grasping her shoulder. After a couple of blinks, she saw a throbbing, crimson vision of her mother standing before her.

"Renna," Alexandria said firmly. "It's all right. You are safe."

Warrenna wiped her brow and told the beast inside her to

go away. *I just fell asleep when I left the great room. We are safe here.*

She sat on a black tile floor, her back propped against a wall. A large kitchen spread out before her, clean white counters and a center-island with a sink. Muffled hums filtered in through the door to the Great Room, and then Warrenna remembered.

The circle of thirteen, hands joined, surrounded Necole's comatose form on the bed. She couldn't say how many hours she chanted with the Orphans, her muscles twitching from the chain of sparks flowing up one arm and down the other. By the time she finally stopped, her knees were wobbly and her calves throbbed.

She yawned. Her back ached from the hard tile that had been her bed. "What time is it, Mom?"

"Nearly ten-thirty." A tall man held her elbow, supporting her. The man, who Warrenna remembered was named Grant, had dark sideburns down to his jaw and the most gorgeous green eyes she had ever seen.

He smiled and bowed his head reverently. Warrenna rolled her eyes.

"How are you feeling?" Alexandria asked.

"Okay, I guess, Mom. I still feel that weird warmth in my fingers."

"Just residue from the cleansing ritual. It's harmless, and will fade in time." She gestured for Grant to help her daughter to her feet.

Warrenna refused his hand and rose on her own. "How's Necole?"

Alexandria looked away and drew her lips together. "Not much better. I'm afraid we just postponed the inevitable. Tamara is still working on her, but your aunt is distracted by something that has come up regarding your friend."

"You mean Thomas?"

Alexandria nodded. "Vincent saw something in his trance,

and Tamara agrees that it needs to be investigated right away. But she can't leave Necole. Do you think Thomas would come here if you asked?"

Warrenna frowned. She pictured Thomas surrounded by Orphans like Grant who treated her like some kind of freaky savior. Then there was the chanting in the next room. "What's wrong?" she asked. "Can't you tell me what's wrong?"

"We're not entirely sure."

Warrenna folded her arms. "Tell me, or I won't ask him."

"Very well." Alexandria shifted her weight to lean more on Grant. "We don't want to alarm him, but Vincent saw suggestions in Thomas's mind that didn't appear to belong. There are signs that someone or something is trying to control his thoughts. Tamara should be able to tell what has him just by looking at him."

Warrenna's heart caught in her throat. "Do you think it's a vampire?"

Alexandria shrugged her narrow shoulders. "I suppose it could be. It takes a powerful creature to influence humans like this. But Bascomville is a quiet area. That's why we moved there."

Warrenna ground her teeth. She didn't want to pull Thomas into her world of hiding, passwords and worrying about what supernatural beast held a grudge against her family. *But it sounds like he might already be here.*

"He's probably very confused right now," Alexandria said. "And if a vampire is responsible, Thomas will be suffering some unexplainable mental anguish."

"Fine," Warrenna relented. "But let's say he *is* under something's control. Are we going to help him get out of it?"

Alexandria's frail body shook through a coughing fit. "Of course." she finally said. "If we must, we will kill whatever is controlling him. We owe him that much for helping you."

"All right, I'll call. I think I left my phone in my bag."

But Alexandria handed her a different phone. "His number is already dialed. Just hit Send."

* * *

Thomas slumped onto the couch. *What I need is a basketball game.*

He clicked the TV on, untucked his shirt, put his feet up and prepared to spend an hour or two thinking about something other than vampires, angels, or dreams.

He found a game competitive enough to keep his attention and relaxed for a few minutes. That is, until a pretty cheerleader with blonde hair came on the screen.

"Oh, crap! Mariah! I was supposed to drive her home last night!"

His headache flared up again with a thump. *She's probably furious with me.*

Thomas hauled himself out of the couch and plodded to the kitchen. He had to call Mariah right then. Better now than a scene at school tomorrow.

As he reached for the phone, it rang, startling him. Maybe Mariah was calling already. *Time to face the music.* He swallowed hard as he picked up the receiver.

"Hi Thomas, it's Renna. How are ya?"

"Um..." He was relieved that it wasn't Mariah ready with a tongue-lashing, but he wasn't ready to deal with the supernatural again.

"Feeling weird?" Warrenna continued. "Confused? Wondering how or why you did some strange things yesterday?"

His eyes widened. "Wow, have you been watching me or something?"

"Er, uh..."

Hey, for once I caught her off-guard.

"It's hard to explain," Warrenna said, "but we saw something that might account for what you went through. Remember the lady with the orange glasses? That's my Aunt Tammy. She wants to see you as soon as possible, but we need to stay here. Could you come to Maldecido this afternoon?"

"I suppose. What does she think is wrong?"

"She's not sure, but we know it's something, uh, unnatural."

Thomas took a deep breath. Then he remembered the sermon Derek O'Neal had given that morning. "Tell you what. I'll go up there if you answer my questions about you and your family."

"Sure. Hold on."

Thomas heard some muffled voices, and then Warrenna came back on. "My mother says I can't go into too much detail over the phone."

"Uh-huh." Thomas chewed on his cheek. He supposed he could just drive there and ask his questions when he arrived. But could he really trust them?

Well, they haven't asked me for anything until now. And if they wanted to kidnap me, they certainly could've done it when I was alone in Tebon Canyon.

He decided to at least play along until he knew what they found in his sample. But he made a mental note to refuse any refreshments they might offer him.

"How about this," he said. "I'll just drive up, and you answer my questions when I get there. Okay?"

"That'll be fine. Do you know where the Foothills Mall is?"

"Yeah, it's got a couple of athletic-shoe stores."

"Okay, good." He heard Warrenna whispering to someone, then she said, "You're gonna go to the parking lot in front of Sears. A gray car with a round yellow sticker on the back bumper will be parked there. You're gonna ask the woman in the driver's seat if she knows how to get to Albert's Spear Shop. She'll say 'Buy a ticket to Berlin.' Got that?"

Thomas scribbled the words onto a Post-it. "Yeah. But why the song and dance?"

"Let's just say that not everybody is happy with what we do."

"I see."

She chuckled. "I doubt it. But maybe you will after you get here. Can you leave soon?"

"Yeah, I'm out the door now. Be up there in about an hour."

"Okay. Drive safe."

Thomas hung up, then stared at the phone as if it were a geometry test. There was still Mariah. He dialed quickly, unsure of what he was going to say, other than that he was a jerk, and he was sorry.

After five rings, an answering machine picked up. Thomas sighed in relief. It was only a temporary reprieve, but at least he wouldn't have to answer any questions just then.

He apologized for being an inconsiderate jerk, then said he would be home in the evening if she wanted to talk. Then he jumped into the Beatermobile and turned the ignition.

As he pumped the gas pedal, he thought about what he was about to do—leave town by himself to hang out with some vampires. *I feel like I should leave a note or something.* He laughed. *Dear Mom and Dad: I went to Maldecido to find out what unnatural thing is happening to me. Please call the National Guard if I'm not back by dinner.*

But it was far too late to explain everything to his parents. They would never believe him anyway.

No, this was *his* decision. *Which means I get all the credit if this turns out to be the best choice I've ever made.*

And all the blame if things go wrong.

Chapter 13

Thomas carefully weaved the Beatermobile amongst the tractor-trailers as he drove north on Interstate 19. The outside temperature climbed as the mountains shrunk away to the horizon, and pale-green prongs of saguaro cacti began to appear along the road.

The familiar drive passed quickly as he tried to think of the properly worded questions for Warrenna. *So, are you guys a drug cult?* felt a little too confrontational.

He turned off the freeway and onto the wide, hectic streets of Maldecido. The traffic flowed much faster than on Bascomville's sleepy roads, but Thomas knew his route and stuck to the lanes he needed.

The Foothills Mall parking lot was busy with scurrying Sunday-afternoon shoppers, and Thomas needed a couple of passes to find the gray car with the yellow bumper sticker.

A woman sat in the driver's seat. Her blond hair was flat and stringy, and large plastic sunglasses rested on her creased, leathery face.

He tapped on the window, and the woman rolled it down an inch. "Do you know where Albert's Spear Shop is?" Thomas asked. "Er, how to get there?"

"Yeah, buy a ticket to Berlin. Get in."

Thomas opened the passenger door and was hit with the aroma of deep-fried cigarettes. The car's vinyl upholstery was cracked and the dashboard carried a thick layer of desert dust and ash.

"So you're Thomas. Name's Terri Jenkins. Here's my mark."

She rolled up her right sleeve, exposing a tattoo on her tanned arm. The design, about the size of a drink coaster, consisted of a black hourglass in a red circle, the inverse of the markings found on a black widow spider.

"That's, uh, kind of creepy," Thomas said.

"Jesus, nobody's told you about the black glass?" Terri shook her head. "It's the mark of Zera. It means I'm friendly to the Orphans."

Thomas remembered the sketches in Warrenna's living room: hourglasses and flames. He didn't understand what "Orphans" meant, but he didn't want to seem stupid.

"So," he said, "you're not, ya know, one of *them*?"

She laughed and started the car. "Honey, with a tan like this? I don't think so. I'm a norm. I just help 'em out when they need stuff done in the daytime. I'd do anything for the Orphans. I'd-a been fanger-food for sure if it weren't for Alex and Rick." She smiled at him. "That's Alexandria and Richard, in case you don't know. Fine folks."

Terri backed the car out of the parking space and drove out of the lot, then turned onto a street heading north, toward some jagged brown mountains.

"I hear you've got some questions, and Alex told me I could tell you anything you wanted to know." She checked the rearview mirror. "We got some time, so fire away."

"Okay." It was easy to come up with his first question: "Why do you call them Orphans?"

"That's what they call themselves." Terri rolled her window down a crack and lit a cigarette. "It's like their parents are the vampires who wanted 'em to feed on us humans, sleep in coffins, live forever, all that stuff. But the Orphans rejected that life. In some cases, they've even killed the vamps that made 'em."

"So they kill vampires?"

She tapped her cigarette against the edge of the window. "Yeah, Alex and Rick hunted down the fangers that made 'em in the hopes that killing the originals would undo the curse. Like in the movies." She shrugged her shoulders. "No dice, though. Once you've got the curse, you've got the curse. So now they hunt down any fanger, find the poor saps the vamps have infected, and let those saps know that they can fight the curse through Zera. See, there's this window. Ten days between getting infected and going full-vamp. If the Orphans find somebody in that window, then that person can fight the curse with their help."

That sounded noble enough to Thomas. "Okay, but how do they fight it? And who is this Zera you keep mentioning?"

Terri gasped, and the car swerved onto the shoulder. She laughed as she steered back on to the road. "So I get to be the one to tell the kid about Zera."

She turned onto a smaller residential road. The mountains slowly filled the horizon as they drew closer. Thomas figured there couldn't be much city remaining this far north.

"Okay kid, here's the deal. The Orphans ain't exactly human, and they ain't exactly vampires either. They've found a way to stay in-between. And that way begins and ends with Zera. She's a goddess. One that nobody's worshipped for a really long time. And there's this ritual that they do called the cleansing."

"Wait." Thomas's jaw hung agape. "A *goddess?*"

"That's the best way to describe her. She's not your fire-

and-brimstone, chuck-lightning-bolts-from-the-clouds sorta deal. From what I hear, she's a little more subtle. Seems she's only available for conversation if you're infected."

They reached a dirt road that traveled around the base of what Thomas now recognized as Mount Maldecido, the tallest peak of the Santa Lupita Range. The mountain's face was sheer and black, as though the many forest fires that charred the summit had somehow burned the cliffs beneath it.

"So," Thomas said, forcing his lips to make the words, "the Orphans worship this goddess."

Terri nodded, downshifting as the small car bounced along the rough road. "Alex's father discovered Zera in some books a while back. If the Orphans follow the cleansing ritual, they go into this trance. Zera then speaks to them and burns some of the curse out of their blood for a while. The cleansing's supposed to be really painful. Like their blood gets lit on fire. But that controls their craving for human blood. Makes them more resistant to sunlight. Basically makes them less of a vampire. It's only temporary, so they have to do the ritual pretty regular."

Thomas couldn't believe this lady was talking so casually about a god. *Well, if they're really vampires, and I might be an angel, why shouldn't there be this Zera?*

Then he remembered the vision at practice, the one of Warrenna in flames that gave him the bruise on his jaw. It had to be the cleansing. *But why did I see it?*

The car jerked to a stop. Thomas couldn't see any structures around, just miles of mesquite and saguaro. For a panicked second, he wondered if he was in the wrong car.

"Uh, why are we stopped?"

Terri's eyes were locked on the rearview mirror. "A blue car with a gray hood was tailing us through the city, but I think I lost him."

"Oh." Thomas was only partially relieved. At least it gave

him the opportunity to ask another of his questions. "Who'd be following us?"

Terri took another drag off her cigarette. "Lots of folks don't like what the Orphans do. Vampires, obviously, and their lackeys. Other demon-servants that want to get in good with the fangers. Then you've got your misguided hero-type hunters with a grudge against anything not one-hundred-percent human. And, for obvious reasons, we want to avoid any police sniffing around. They wouldn't be as understanding of the Orphans' curse as you've been." She grinned at him and hit the gas.

They continued in silence as Thomas struggled to absorb the facts Terri had relayed. It seemed to him that the Orphans had a tough time. They hunted vampires without any help from the *norms* they were protecting, all while undergoing a painful purification just to stay somewhat human. And they had to keep it all a secret, because who would believe that Orphans were *good* vampires?

He snorted. *Well, who other than* me *would believe?*

A question came to mind. "Warrenna told me she was born a vampire. Is that common?"

"Hell, no. Vampires can't bear children like humans. But Zera intervened. She commanded that Alex and Rick have a child, and did something godlike to allow Renna to happen."

Tears crept into Thomas's eyes, and the familiar tightness in his throat returned. He tried to stay focused. "But why? Why give someone the curse from birth?"

Terri shrugged her shoulders and turned off the dirt road onto a residential street. They headed toward a large iron gate that blocked the way. She brought the car to a stop beside a guard-booth and turned to her passenger.

"Word is Alex and Rick refused at first. But then they figured there must be a good reason Zera wanted them to do this, even if they couldn't see it just then. Some of the Orphans think it was so Renna could meet you." She winked at him.

Thomas rolled his eyes, but part of him really liked the idea that he and Warrenna had been predestined to meet.

Terri turned to a squawk box in front of the guard booth. "Hiya, Luis. Is that you on day watch again?"

"Yeah," a tired voice came from the speaker. "Somebody's got to do it. Who's that you got with you?"

Thomas leaned forward to see a small security camera hanging from the ceiling of the booth. "This here's Tommy," Terri said. "The one we heard so much about."

"Ah!" Luis said. "*Bíenvenídos, Tómas!* We are happy to have you. Terri, I'll give him a norm-tag for now."

A metal shelf slowly extended from underneath the window, and Terri lifted a laminated slip of paper from it. "Hello, my name is THOMAS" was written on the nametag, as though he were attending a convention. The word NORM appeared in big red letters beneath his name.

"Zera is the way," Luis said, and the gate rolled to the side.

Terri put the car in gear. "We should put a question mark after the *norm*," she said with a grin.

Thomas stuck the tag to his shirt pocket and looked out the window. The modest houses passing by looked like everyday suburban homes. They could have been from his neighborhood, except for one important difference. All the windows were bricked up.

"What is this?" he asked. "A planned community for vampires?"

"Sort of. We call it the Orphanage. All these houses are owned by Orphans, or by friendly norms. It's a safe place where we have meetings, bring the newly Orphaned, stuff like that. All thanks to Rick and Alex. Without the two of them, many Orphans wouldn't have a place to live or a job. Hell, they'd be vampires, running around killing people."

"Orphans have jobs?"

Terri gave him another quizzical look. "Well, yeah. How do you think they pay for things?"

Thomas shook his head. *Hunting vampires, dealing with the curse,* and *holding down a job? Orphans have busy lives.*

"Anyway, we're here."

Terri brought the car to a stop in a cul-de-sac filled with parked vehicles ranging in style and cost. Thomas saw everything from old pickups with faded paint jobs to brand-new SUVs with leather interiors and chrome hubcaps.

"Doesn't this seem weird to you?" Thomas said. "A bunch of vampires out here in the Arizona desert? Can you think of a sunnier place in the world?"

Terri smiled again and extinguished her cigarette in the ashtray. "Well, kid, where's the last place you'd look for a vampire?"

Antarctica. But she has a point.

He followed Terri up a sidewalk to the largest house in the cul-de-sac. Every section of the residence had at least two stories, even the three-car garage. Gray columns supported what amounted to an extended eave, as though someone built a gazebo roof over the front yard and connected the covering to the main building. The lack of windows reminded Thomas of a large power station, or a hardened military compound.

Terri noticed her companion's nervous glances and patted Thomas on the back. "Relax, kid. You're in the safest place in the world right now. And from what I've heard, you might be a major player in the future of everyone in there. Rick and Alex will make damn certain nothing happens to you, and I have a feeling Renna will too."

Terri gave the door a couple of solid knocks. It opened quickly, and there stood Richard. He wore his customary blank expression, but Thomas could see dark patches of skin beneath his eyes.

Richard gave them a split-second smile. "Ah, Thomas. Thank you for coming. Terri, we are in your debt as always."

She waved her hand. "Ah, it ain't nothin'. I gave Tommy here the scoop on the Orphans, so he's a little freaked out, but he's a good kid. Be nice to him." She smacked her forehead and added, "And, oh, I'm gonna go tell Luis to watch out for a blue sedan with a gray hood."

Richard frowned. "Was someone following you?"

"I think so. I lost him back in the city, though. Didn't see him once I reached the mountains."

She turned to Thomas. "I'll be back in a little while to give you a ride back to your car." Then she leaned in close and whispered, "You'll get used to the vampire thing. Inside, they're just people like us. Well, like *me*, anyway."

She smiled and turned away, and Richard beckoned Thomas to come inside.

Thomas followed the vampire down a dim, cool hallway. The conditions reminded him of Warrenna's house in Bascomville, and Thomas guessed that being cursed affected the body. The Orphans probably wanted every place they went to feel like a Transylvanian castle.

They passed a set of partially open double-doors, and a bright line of light caught Thomas's attention. A quick glance revealed a bed and an IV stand. "Excuse me sir," he said. "What's in there?"

Richard stopped and squinted. "Ah. That's where we are keeping our injured compatriot. Something tortured her, and we're trying to keep her from losing her humanity. It's like her assailant *wanted* her to turn."

He looked Thomas in the eye. "You can go in there if you want. She can't hurt you."

Thomas couldn't tell why, but he was curious what an Orphan struggling to stay human looked like. "Okay, I think I will."

The walls of the room stretched around him in an enormous square, and once again, Thomas found himself surrounded by representations of hourglasses and flame. The mark of Zera was repeated over and over again in oil paintings, charcoal sketches, ink drawings, even in fired-bronze sculptures.

The only furniture consisted of the bed, in the exact center of the room, the accompanying IV stand, and a small folding chair. Thomas approached the bed as quietly as he could, but his sneakers made hard sounds on the dark tile floor.

On first glance, Thomas suspected the body on the bed to be a corpse. The woman's ashen skin was pulled tight around her high-boned cheeks, her thick lips were chapped, and a long white scar ran from her left eyebrow up into her short curly hair. But her narrow torso did eventually rise and fall. She was still alive, if barely.

Warmth grew in Thomas's chest as he watched the woman breathe, and his fingertips felt as though each one housed a moth, eager to float his fingernails to the fluorescent light above.

Vampire or not, she's obviously suffered.

"This is Necole," Richard's voice came from behind him. "She was one of the strongest of us. Something went to great care to make her bleed for a long time." He shook his head. "There are other, much faster ways to turn an Orphan into a vampire. We can only conclude that whatever did this to her wanted to watch her suffer."

Thomas's breath came slowly, and his legs were coiled springs. The warmth spread up into his neck.

Poor soul. I wish I could ease your pain.

His eyes rolled upward, and he reached out to Necole's forehead. He felt a tiny spark when he touched her, and then she was gone.

Chapter 14

There was no bed anymore. In its place was a heavy stone slab.

Thomas turned around. Richard was gone, and the room looked drastically different. The walls were no longer covered with the mark of Zera. Instead, they were draped with a gray cottony substance that partially reflected some bluish light. The light seemed to originate from behind Thomas, but when he turned he saw no light source, just another puffy wall. The air smelled musty and old.

He took a step toward the downy material, and the bluish light intensified. He could now see that the stuff covering the walls was actually layer after layer of spider web. Hundreds of black spiders, some as big as his fist, scurried from his sight.

One sprang toward him, and Thomas put his hand up to shield his face. But his hand didn't rise. Instead, a giant bluish-white flame swung from his shoulder and intercepted the spider mid-flight, obliterating every speck of the creature.

So I'm the light source. Now this is interesting!

Thomas moved his flickering limb forward, and the flame

pressed into the cobwebs, instantly burning out the silky material. He turned his shoulder and the flame arced, burning a wide slash into the gossamer curtain.

He took a few paces, dragging his flaming hand along the wall. A wavy pattern of scorched rock followed him. He moved his other hand, which was also flame. Thomas burned parallel lines into the wall, and he rejoiced in every evaporated arachnid.

He tried to spell his name, but the webbing burned too fast. When he stopped to admire his attempt, he heard the humming.

The noise was soft and high-pitched, and was loudest around the stone slab. Upon inspecting the block, Thomas found that it was actually shaped like a huge stone coffin.

On a whim, he pressed his flames against the side of the lid. The slab easily slid off and landed on the floor with a thump.

With the lid off, the hum became louder, so Thomas peeked inside the coffin.

A dozen hairy spiders the size of cats squirmed in a knot of legs and beady eyes. Thomas could hear the clattering of dozens of tiny teeth gnashing together.

And then the spiders leapt at him.

In a panic, he waved his flames. One of the eight-legged monsters passed under his left arm and readied to sink its huge pincers into his leg.

But just as the spider touched his skin, the hairy beast evaporated with a *poof!*

Thomas smiled, amazed. *Right on.* He hunted down the rest of the freakish bugs and bathed each of them in his flame. But still the whine reached his ears.

He looked back into the coffin to investigate. Webbing was fluffed to the brim, so he swept one of his glowing flames along the top, burning the web away in an even pattern. The hum became louder.

Another pass revealed a layer of tightly spun web. Thomas

held the flame on the same spot for a few moments to dig a little hole. He drew a line in this way, like a blowtorch through sheet metal.

A face appeared in the line, and Necole's dark eyes looked up at him in abject terror. The whine wasn't a whine at all. It was her piercing scream.

Hands pulled on his chest and shoulders, and Thomas stumbled backward. His vision went fuzzy for a moment, and in a blink, the coffin was the bed again. People swarmed around Necole's screaming form.

Richard's angry face was clenched before him, and the vampire's strong hands gripped Thomas's shoulders.

"Get the hell away from her!"

He shoved Thomas into a door that opened behind him as he fell.

Thomas landed on hard tile. Richard followed him through the door, and Thomas scrambled to get to his feet while scooting away.

"What did you do to her?" Richard demanded.

"I don't know!" Thomas wheezed as he struggled for breath. "I was in a cave, and there were spiders everywhere, so I was burning them, with like my hand or something, and the lady was in the coffin…"

"You leave him alone!"

Warrenna stood at Thomas's side, glaring defiantly at her father. "You invited him, remember? Anything that happened in there is *your* fault, not his!"

Richard growled and plunged back into the great room. As the door closed Thomas heard shouting, dragging furniture, and, above everything else, Necole's panicked screams.

Warrenna took a deep breath and looked down at Thomas. "Nobody told me you were here. I probably wasn't supposed to know. Are you all right?"

Thomas nodded, and took a second to catch his breath. His

back was propped against a center island of a kitchen. The cabinets and countertops gleamed antiseptic white in contrast to the black tile.

He winced as he recalled Necole's fearful eyes. "I don't know what happened in there. I just wanted to make her feel better, but I somehow ended up in a cave or something. I don't know if I was hallucinating or what."

"It's so typical," Warrenna spat, but then she caught herself. "Sorry. Not you. My parents. They didn't tell me they wanted you here to see if you could help Necole. But it's obvious they did. I wonder if Mom made up the story about something being wrong with you. Just to get you here, you know."

Thomas ran his hand through his hair. "I don't think she made anything up about that. Look, should I get out of here while I have the chance? Your dad looked really mad."

"He's got no reason to be. I'm sure that wasn't your fault in there. He should know that a pure soul like yours could never hurt anybody on purpose."

Her cheeks colored, and she looked away. "Anyway, Aunt Tammy probably still wants to see you. But she's bound to be occupied with Necole for a while." She sat down beside him on the floor. "So I can answer those questions you wanted to ask."

Thomas smiled at her embarrassment. *I do like to see her off-guard.* "Actually, your norm friend Terri answered most of them for you. But I have a new one. What's it like worshipping Zera? Does she really talk to you?"

Her eyebrows arched in surprise. "So you know about Zera. Uh, well, I don't...worship her."

Thomas cocked his head. "But I thought that was how Orphans stayed human."

"It is." Warrenna rubbed her wrist. "My parents performed the ritual on me a few times when I was young, and, um, once recently. Because of my, um, special birth, the curse hasn't progressed that far. So I don't really need Zera yet. To be honest, I never want to see her again if I don't have to." She looked at the floor. "She doesn't ever say my name. She just calls me *daughter*."

Thomas touched her shoulder. "So you're saying that you're the daughter of a goddess?"

"No."

Warrenna turned to him, poking a finger at his chest. "Zera may be responsible for my messed-up existence, but she is not my mother."

Thomas looked into her bold gray eyes, and the warmth sparked inside his chest again. His fingers became light as feathers, and his eyes rolled up into his lids.

"And with me," he said, "you won't ever need Zera."

He gently cupped Warrenna's cheek in his hand. Her skin was cool, yet warmth blossomed inside him.

Warrenna looked at him, stunned. But then she pressed her cheek into his hand, welcoming his touch. Her lips touched his wrist, and the air around them shimmered.

And then the door opened, and Thomas drew his hand back like he touched a red-hot stove burner.

Alexandria hobbled in, leaning on a black cane and holding the hand of the woman with the orange-lens glasses.

Warmth swirled inside Thomas, and his vision took a moment to refocus. "Uh, hello, ma'am," he said slowly. "Is Necole okay?"

"She's stable again," Aunt Tammy said. She guided Alexandria to a barstool at the counter. "How she really is, we won't know until Vince can take a sample."

Thomas swallowed hard. "Look, I'm sorry, I don't know what happened."

"Don't feel badly, Thomas." She glanced at Warrenna, then back to him. "You only did what came naturally."

Warrenna blushed again, and edged away from Thomas.

"Right now, I'm more concerned about *your* well-being,

Thomas," Alexandria continued. She gestured to her companion. "Tamara needs to look you over for a moment."

"On your feet, please," Aunt Tammy said. "Look straight up."

Thomas obeyed, and Aunt Tammy ran her fingers along his neck, peering at his skin. "Have you had any blackouts recently? Any time you couldn't account for?"

The vampire's cool touch made Thomas shiver, as did having her teeth so close to his neck. "Actually, yes, on Wednesday. I went from standing in the shower to standing in a hallway at Chiricahua. There's about thirty minutes, maybe more, that I still can't remember."

Aunt Tammy's hands abruptly stopped their probing. She chewed on the knuckle of her index finger. "I know this has been a strange couple of days for you, but I need you to think. During the last week, have you felt compelled to do anything that didn't really make sense, either at the time, or in retrospect?"

Thomas thought for a moment. The curiosity about the paintings seemed natural. The sadness at seeing Warrenna transform was strange, but he didn't remember feeling compelled to do anything….

"Oh yeah," he groaned, remembering. "Yeah, last night. I did something that still feels kinda crazy and stupid."

Warrenna frowned. "What happened?"

Thomas rubbed his neck and looked away. "Well, there's this girl. Mariah, from English class. Anyway, I was at this party with her, and, things were going pretty well, and I had her in my arms, and I saw Renna's eyes somehow. And then I felt terrible, and I couldn't be there anymore. It's weird, I really, you know, wanted to be with this girl. But it felt *wrong*, and I don't know why."

Aunt Tammy winced and looked at Alexandria, but Alexandria was looking at her daughter.

"Warrenna?" Alexandria said. "Is there anything you'd like to tell us?"

Warrenna blinked. "Not really. Why? What's going on?"

"I just thought you might want to explain yourself," Alexandria said. "Because Thomas is acting like he is in your thrall."

"He's what?" Warrenna said at the same time that Thomas sputtered, "I'm what?"

Aunt Tammy nodded, frowning. "He's got the symptoms. The missing time, the rejection of prior desire, and Vince saw unnatural thoughts in his mind."

"It must have happened when you transformed in front of him," Alexandria said. "You don't have any experience with the beast. You probably couldn't help yourself. I didn't know you were capable of enthralling. But then," she sighed, "you've always been full of surprises."

Warrenna shook her head. "No, you're wrong, I didn't *do* anything. I just transformed and transformed back."

"Thrall?"

Everyone looked at Thomas, whose face had lost all color.

"We're afraid so," Aunt Tammy said gently. "Thrall is sort of like being hypnotized. It's how very powerful vampires get humans to do their will. The victim has no awareness of the strings being pulled."

"But I didn't do anything!" Warrenna cried. "Tommy, you were there that night. You believe me, don't you?"

Thomas closed his eyes as he tried to remember the events of the past week. "Yeah," he said evenly. "You transformed on Thursday. I had the missing time on Wednesday."

But all the strangeness began this week. The sadness, the visions, the confusion...

He remembered the blackout, and the image of Warrenna in flames at practice. Then there were the strange hallucinations with her paintings. All of the wrenching sorrow and embarrassing tears happened this week.

And it all began right after he brushed against her arm while passing out a handout in third-hour English.

The drowsy warmth evaporated. His eyes felt like ice cubes in his skull. "Oh my God," he whispered. "You did it to me on Monday."

"No, Thomas," Warrenna said. "I haven't done anything. I swear to you."

"We can't enthrall in our human form," Aunt Tammy added. "And anyway, it wears off as long as you're not around her beast form for around..."

"No," Thomas interrupted. He pointed a finger at Aunt Tammy. "*You* can't do it. You also can't walk around in the sun." He moved the finger to point at Warrenna. "But *she* can."

The bowling ball was back in his torso, reminding him of the moment he first touched Warrenna. The weight was cold and hard, dragging his insides down to the floor. "Oh, God, it's all been a lie. All of it. And I had Mariah in my arms. Jesus, I *ran* from her. Because all I could think about was you."

He fell to his knees. All the dreamy thoughts of being an angel, the elation of the basketball game, the cool, thrilling touch of Warrenna's cheek—all lies. His stomach juices swirled around the bowling ball. Her pulsing red eyes hadn't burned with suffering. They burned with evil.

"You monster," he spat. "You've had me under your spell this whole time."

Tears slipped down Warrenna's face. "No, Tommy. I didn't want any of that, I promise you. I never wanted your life to get all screwed up, that was the last thing I wanted."

"Don't come near me!" he yelled, staggering to his feet. "None of you freaks come near me. You're not getting me under your spell ever again!"

Thomas barged through the door into the great room. A couple of people stood by the bed, and they turned at the sound of the door.

Thomas's heart pounded. They were vampires, too.

He sprinted as fast as he could to the double doors. The vampires didn't react, and he was quickly back in the first dim hallway.

There was the outside door. *If I can get to sunlight, they won't chase me.*

He flung himself at the exit. The door opened easily, but he crashed right into Terri. They both crumpled to the ground.

That was when Thomas remembered that he was trapped in a gated neighborhood, miles away from civilization. He didn't even know which direction to go to find the Beatermobile.

"Terri," he gasped, "I'm sorry, uh, could you take me to my car? I'm ready to go."

Terri climbed to her feet. "Sure, honey. But what happened? You're whiter than the cursed folk. What's got you so spooked?"

What if she's under some vampire's thrall like I just was? "Nothing. It's just creepy being around so many of them. Can we go?"

She shrugged. "Well, all right, let's go." Her eyes looked past Thomas toward the door. "That okay with you?"

Thomas slowly turned to find Richard standing in the doorway. The vampire's arms were folded, and he glared at Thomas with an expression that chilled the young man's heart.

Run, get to sunlight!

But Thomas's legs were frozen in place.

"He is no prisoner here," Richard said coldly. "If he wants to go, that's fine with me."

Thomas sighed heavily. "Okay then," he said, and backed away.

Thomas glanced over his shoulder on every third step as he and Terri walked to her car. He thought he could feel Warrenna's eyes on his back, like two invisible lasers boring into his shoulder blades.

But as the distance between him and the Orphanage grew, the feeling became weaker and weaker.

He told Terri about the strange vision with Necole, and that it really frightened him and he just wanted to go home and get some rest. Terri assured him that he would get used to bizarre things happening, and he made a big deal of just needing a little more time to deal with all the world-changing stuff he heard today.

All lies, of course. He just wanted to get to his car, and never see another vampire in his entire life.

They finally reached the Foothills Mall parking lot, and Thomas had never been happier to see the Beatermobile's dusty white paint. He waved goodbye to Terri with a fake smile. As soon as she drove away, he began to shake.

He gripped the steering wheel and took several deep breaths, feeling lucky to still be alive. He considered going to the police, but he doubted they would believe anything he said. He pictured a bored officer rolling his eyes. "Of course they're vampires," he would say. "Hell, I'm a zombie, and over there's my buddy the Wolf-Man. He's a little hairy, but otherwise a good guy."

He rubbed his forehead and wondered how many stupid things he did while under Warrenna's spell. He was angry with himself for being fooled for so long, but a week ago he thought vampires were just legend. How could he have known what he was in for?

In his rearview mirror he caught a glimpse of the long shadows being cast by the enormous buildings of the Foothills Mall. He realized he had to get farther away from the Orphanage before the sun went down. Terri might tell them where he was.

When he reached the interstate, he floored the accelerator. Then he peeled the nametag off his shirt, ripped it in half, and threw the pieces out the window.

Stupid of me to think I was an angel. I'm just an ordinary guy who has weird dreams.

He retrieved the paper heart from the glove compartment and flung it outside. It caught an updraft, and disappeared into the desert sky.

Tiny cars and trucks moved south in the distance as Warrenna watched the interstate. She knew Thomas was inside one of those little dots. And he was thanking his lucky stars that he got away from her.

The long shadows told her that the sun was close to setting behind looming Mount Maldecido. But still she paced along the tall stucco wall that circled the perimeter of the house, allowing the rays to sting her face. *Figures. The only place I can be alone is where we burn.*

"Renna."

Warrenna glanced over her shoulder and saw her mother standing by the heavy wooden gate. Another step and Alexandria would be awash in sunlight.

"You should come inside, Renna. You know this is bad for you."

Warrenna turned back to watch the distant highway. "I know how much I can take."

"It's not as bad as you think."

"He hates me, Mom!" Warrenna cried to the desert. "He thinks I got inside his head. That I'm controlling him. He was my only way out of this life, and thanks to your scene back there, now he's afraid of me!" By the time she finished speaking, Warrenna was choking back sobs.

Alexandria put her hands on her hips. "Don't kid yourself, Warrenna Rachel. There can be no doubt that you somehow put him in your thrall. The evidence is too strong." Her voice softened. "But you shouldn't feel badly about it. We all know enthralling him wasn't your intention. If anything, it's my fault for not giving you enough of an appreciation for how dangerous we are when in our other form. And you know I had to tell him. We're no better than the fiends if we don't tell our human friends what we know."

Warrenna smiled ruefully. *I hate it when she's right.* "You know, it figures," she said quietly. "My intentions, as usual, are meaningless. They always have been. I didn't mean to, but I pulled him into our world. I didn't mean to, but I enthralled the only boy I reached out to. He's right to be scared."

Warrenna bowed her head, and her heart sank into her stomach. "Because inside, I'm really a monster. It's all I've ever been, and it's all I'll ever be now that he's gone."

Tears rushed to her eyes, but she was sick of them. They didn't suit a fiend like her.

Suddenly her face was buried in her mother's chest. She felt Alexandria's heart slowly thud through her cheekbone.

"You are no monster," her mother's voice softly came. "You are my daughter. You are strong, and you are beautiful."

Warrenna looked up to see Alexandria's small, steady smile, and tears flooded her vision. She sobbed into her mother's shoulder, and Alexandria stroked the back of her head like she had so many years ago. Back when there was no curse, just something called *different.* They held each other tightly, but only for a moment. Warrenna could still feel the sting of sunlight on the back of her neck.

She backed away in alarm, knowing how dangerous this was for Alexandria. "Mom, the sun."

But she saw only a sliver of orange glowing above the black mountain. Mount Maldecido's shadow didn't yet encompass her, but completely shaded her mother. Warrenna sighed and returned to the comfort of the embrace.

Alexandria wiped Warrenna's tears with her thumb. "You know, Renna, if there's one thing I've learned in my time in our world, it's that fate is a powerful force. It's what drove Warren, your grandfather and namesake, to search for a cure for the terrible curse that had befallen me. And fate will make Thomas curious as to what and why he really is."

Alexandria turned, bringing her daughter into the safety of the shadow. "When we return to Bascomville, give Thomas space. Don't initiate contact. You'll see. He'll realize that you didn't mean to enthrall him. He'll also see that most of what you two share has nothing to do with what happened today."

They stopped to pass through the heavy wooden gate and Alexandria carefully replaced the thick padlock over the latch.

"He'll come back to you," she said. "And it won't be because you want him to. He'll find you again because he wants to know what his fate truly is."

Warrenna sniffled and nodded. *It might take a while. He'll probably spread a story around Chiricahua about how weird I am.*

They re-entered the cool darkness of the kitchen. "Do you think he'll keep our secret?" Warrenna asked.

"I think he knows no one would believe him."

A shout came from behind the swinging great-room door. "Don't go in there! You should go back to your bed!"

Alexandria stopped. "Necole?"

Then Necole appeared in the doorway, fighting off Aunt Tammy and Richard as she went. Her skin was dark as chocolate, and her big eyes carried an alarming intensity.

"Where is he?" she demanded. Her voice was rich and clear as she strode toward them. "Where is the boy?"

"Thomas is gone," Alexandria said as Necole neared. Even though Necole towered over a foot above her, she met the woman's flashing gaze unwaveringly. "He is not to be touched. He is far too important in the big picture."

"I don't want to hurt him."

A grin split Necole's mouth from ear to ear, revealing her gleaming white teeth. "I want to *thank* him. He freed me from my nightmare."

Alexandria's mouth hung open in surprise. She glanced to Aunt Tammy in the doorway, who shrugged her shoulders.

Warrenna took the opportunity to speak. "Necole. Are you cured?"

Necole shook her head. "The beast still prowls inside me. But I feel better than I've felt in years." She clasped her hands on the shoulders of both mother and daughter. "When do you think I could see him again? I simply must thank him."

Warrenna gave a weak smile. "It might be a little while. And I'm afraid that's my fault."

Chapter 15

Finished with his transcription, Thomas closed the journal, jumped from the desk and threw open his bedroom window. The morning sun shone warmly on his face, and a nest of wrens sang from a mesquite tree in the gravel yard. He took a deep breath of crisp air.

A new week, a new beginning.

He took a quick cold shower to get his blood moving, then pulled on his white Arizona Cardinals t-shirt and climbed into his favorite blue jeans. Breakfast was a wheat bagel, a banana, and a tall glass of orange juice. He wanted to have plenty of energy as he took on the new week.

After making sure that crucifixes were ensconced near every possible entrance to the house, he slept well the previous night. His mind was clear of questions as to how human he truly was, and he looked forward to getting back to his quiet, easy life. Sure, there might be vampires out there, but now that he knew about them, he could be prepared. So what if nobody would believe him?

As he stepped into the bathroom for the daily struggle with his hair, Thomas thought about the story he would give his friends: that new girl really messed with his head, made him doubt who he really was and who his friends really were. But he figured out her game and told her off. He was feeling much better now.

After that, he would ask to get filled in on what happened at the party after he left, and otherwise act as normal as he could.

He cringed when he thought of the damage he might have done to his relationship with Mariah. She didn't call back, so he figured she must be mad. *Maybe I should buy her some flowers. They'd be a good start, anyway.*

The doorbell rang, and for a moment, Thomas was afraid that Warrenna might be waiting on the other side of the door, ready to enthrall him again. But that was silly. It was probably just Brendan. He practiced his story one more time, raced to the door and opened it.

Standing on the welcome mat was Derek O'Neal, dressed in his customary white suit. "Hello, Thomas," he said pleasantly. "Are your parents home?"

Thomas blinked. "Uh, no. My dad's at work, and my mom took my brother to get his allergy shots."

"I see." O'Neal removed his white fedora. "Well, that will make this easier."

"Make what easier?"

"Capturing their son, the vampire-lackey."

The old man lunged forward, thrusting the open hole of his hat toward Thomas's head. Thomas stumbled back, and the darkness of the fedora covered his face.

The hat was home to a powerfully sour stench. Thomas gagged, and plunged into a deep sleep.

* * *

Whump!

Thomas's cheek pressed into sticky vinyl. An automobile engine growled in his ears, alongside the whistle of air conditioning. The awful smell was still in his nose, like slivers embedded in his nostrils.

As he recovered his senses, he found that his hands were bound behind him, and he felt gravity gently pressing him into the seat, the familiar feeling of a car in motion. His forehead throbbed, and his shoulder ached from his awkward position.

He dug his foot into the floorboard and hauled himself upright. The effort made him dizzy and nauseous. O'Neal's short white hair stood above the headrest of the driver's seat, and a look out the window revealed desert brush passing by. He also saw that he was sitting in a blue car with a gray hood, the colors of the car that followed Terri in Maldecido.

"Where are you taking me?" Thomas gasped.

"You're in luck, boy," O'Neal said without turning around. "You will have your blood purified before you meet the Creator. Perhaps then He will forgive your sinful vampire collaborations."

The sour smell faded as Thomas coughed, but the dizziness remained. His brain seemed to spin on a turntable mounted inside his neck while the rest of his body remained still. "What do you mean vampires? There's no such thing."

"You can lose the act, boy. I know you were in their Maldecido compound all day yesterday. And you hung around the half-breed project all last week. What did they say they would give you? Power? Eternal youth? Well, all their empty promises end today."

Thomas thought quickly. O'Neal seemed to know about the Orphans, and hadn't just followed him in Maldecido. But what was a half-breed project? Whatever it was, he had to talk fast.

"I'm not with them anymore, sir," he said. "I mean, I think I was under some kind of spell, but I'm out of it now."

O'Neal snorted, flashing a toothy grin in the rearview mirror. "You're lying. But even if you aren't, it doesn't matter. I need you to draw them out."

Thomas bit his cheek, which tasted like vomit and car exhaust. He thought maybe his ribcage had collapsed around his heart, for every beat seemed to verge on exploding though his chest. Being enthralled might have been confusing and creepy, but it didn't come close to being kidnapped.

"I know you can't betray your masters," O'Neal continued, his voice eerily cheerful. "But don't worry. You won't have to do anything but bleed."

Thomas's throat tightened. Now, he recognized the scorched pavement of Carter Avenue. They were headed west, where the mesquite and barbed wire faded to dust and thistle. They were headed away from help.

Thomas swallowed hard, and was unable to keep his voice from quavering. "Look, sir, I'll be honest with you. I'm not entirely sure what's going on here, but I really don't think I'm evil. And I don't think God would be too happy with you just killing me."

"As though you could know the thoughts of the Creator." O'Neal sneered into the rearview mirror. "Boy, I don't know what your story is. Your skin doesn't burn from my holy garments." He held up an arm to show the sleeve of his white suit-jacket. "But the vampires treat you like one of their own. That means the fiends want you for something, and that makes you good bait for my trap."

Thomas coughed again. *So much for the truth setting me free.* "But these vampires are different," he continued, though he wasn't sure if it was true. "They *fight* the curse. They don't hunt people, they hunt vampires. They're on our side."

O'Neal shook his head and laughed. "Sure they are. What else did they tell you? That they're searching for a cure? Or maybe that they worship some fire god that controls their blood-cravings? I'll bet they ended up getting some blood from you anyway."

"Actually no, they never did."

But then he remembered Friday evening at Warrenna's house. "Uncle Vince," the older man with the wandering blue gaze. "We need to see what you really are," he said, and then took a vial of Thomas's blood.

His stomach flip-flopped. *Was that what all this has been about?*

"The vampires have many alluring stories they tell to ensnare children like you," O'Neal continued, his voice rising. "They know how to make you feel special. To make your ordinary lives feel exciting and important. That's what they did to Jimmy. My poor little brother needed so badly to identify with something."

Thomas saw the man's face scrunch up in the rearview mirror. He pounded the steering wheel. "He was an easy target!" he cried, tears spilling down his cheeks. "I'm so sorry, Jimmy. I should have talked you out of coming to this godforsaken desert. But don't you worry. I've got another one of them here in the car with me. And he's gonna lead me to more. I'll kill every last one of them for what they did to you."

Thomas swallowed hard. O'Neal was definitely a few bricks shy of a load, and talking to him wasn't going to help anything. But he went back to what O'Neal said about blood. *If this was all about getting my blood, then why did Warrenna's family only take that one vial? And why tell me I was in the thrall? They had to know I'd react.*

His head pounded as he searched for answers. O'Neal's description felt frighteningly accurate, but his credibility wasn't the greatest. And Thomas knew he hadn't done anything to deserve getting killed.

The car turned onto a bumpy dirt road, and Thomas slumped against a door. He watched the mountains in the distance and tried to remember the angle of the sun.

We have to stop sometime. I'll make a run for it then. I'll get back to Carter Avenue and flag somebody down. Border Patrol drives around here all the time. They'll help me.

The road curved behind a hill, from south to west again. At the foot of a low mountain range sat a dusty building with arched windows and a flat roof. The arched doorway reminded Thomas of St. Stephen's.

Then he remembered the stories about an abandoned church in the middle of nowhere that the football team used as a drinking destination. Brendan once called it the Mission.

As the car pulled closer, Thomas saw heaps of old beer cans, bottles, ammunition shells and other trash scattered in the desert. The road ended a few feet in front of the building, and O'Neal brought the car to a stop there, exited the car and slammed the door.

Thomas took a deep breath and steeled himself to fight through the pain and dizziness as soon as his captor opened one of the back doors to let him out.

But O'Neal walked away toward the Mission, leaving Thomas to bake inside the car.

A few minutes later, O'Neal emerged again. Now, he wore a black gas mask. He stopped a few feet from the car and looked at his wristwatch.

Pop–psshhhhh.

A tiny white valve popped up from the center console and began spewing a greenish mist. The familiar sour smell filled Thomas's nostrils again, so he held his breath. Desperate, he pulled at the door handle with his bound hands, but the latch went flush, as though locked from the outside. He kicked at the windows, but they were solid.

He took a deep, strangled breath and blacked out.

* * *

Rocks dug into his back. He was being dragged across some dirt. Or gravel, maybe.

He struggled, but his heavy limbs were useless. He fought his eyes open, but all he could see was shadowy haze.

Thomas felt himself being pulled up, then pushed down into a hard chair, draping his bound arms around the back. He felt a pinch in one shin, and then the other. As he sluggishly reacted to the pain, he discovered that his legs were tied to the chair. He took a breath and pressure dug into his sides and across his navel. That meant a rope bound him there as well.

Thomas blinked a few times. Four small, cracked, dusty pews stood before him. Beams of bright yellow light shone through spaces where windows once stood, and through gaping holes in the roof. The interior of the Mission was barely larger than his bedroom, and reeked of beer and ash. Even so, those scents were welcome after that awful gas.

Pain suddenly stabbed his left arm. He looked to find O'Neal withdrawing a hypodermic needle.

"What now," Thomas mumbled.

"Anti-coagulants," O'Neal said. He dropped the syringe into a black briefcase and retrieved a different needle. "Can't have you clotting up on me."

The old man jabbed the new needle into Thomas's left arm, just at the pit of his elbow.

"The more you struggle, the more it will hurt." O'Neal placed the plunger into the needle's housing and drew the handle back. Dark blood quickly filled the plastic tube. With a satisfied grunt, O'Neal attached a clear plastic hose to the end of the tube. The other end of the hose dropped down beside the chair into a shiny silver bucket.

Crimson shot down the hose, and Thomas heard a quick

tapping as his blood dripped into the bucket. He tried to wriggle the needle out of his arm, but he could barely move in the chair, and his thrashing only made the wound hurt more.

Pain chased the gas away, allowing fear and panic to grip Thomas's thoughts. "Why don't you just kill me?"

"Oh, no," O'Neal said with a twisted grin. He pulled a cellular phone from his white blazer. "No, I need you alive for a little while longer."

The old man pressed a button on his phone and held it to his ear. "Hello, Richard," he said cheerfully, then listened a moment. "How I got your number is hardly relevant. I believe I have a friend of yours here."

O'Neal held the phone up to Thomas's face as he jabbed the needle with his other hand. Thomas yelped, and O'Neal put the phone back to his ear.

"Yes, Mister Thomas Gelbaugh sits here filling my holy pail with his scrumptious blood. If you want him to live, I suggest you come to the abandoned mission off Connolly Ranch Road with your half-breed daughter. Straight-up trade, no tricks. Oh, and you'd better hurry. I don't think he can bleed like this for more than another hour."

He listened for a moment. "Then you can collect his corpse at your leisure. But I warn you, I'm going to keep all his blood for my traps." He clicked the phone shut and slipped it back into his blazer.

The tapping from the bucket ceased, but Thomas knew that blood dripping onto blood was quieter than blood dripping onto metal.

"You really thought Richard would trade his own daughter for me?" he said.

"Heavens, no. Richard will make *sure* the half-breed doesn't come within a hundred miles of here. But if your blood is as delicious as I suspect, he will come after you himself."

The old man took a couple of steps across the room and lifted a thin piece of plywood against one of the glassless windows. "He'll probably bring his fiend of a wife, too." He hammered some nails into the wood. "They're the only vampires close enough to get here before you dry up. They'll run right into my trap."

He giggled as he hung a crucifix on one of the nails. "And then I'll have exterminated two of the most powerful vampires in the region and shattered the organization of their little clan. The half-breed will be ripe for the picking."

Thomas squinted. "You mean Renna? What's so big about her?"

O'Neal stopped his hammering and focused his beady blue eyes on his captive. His voice quieted to a hush. "She is the new breed, little boy. Your girlfriend is more powerful than any vampire I've ever seen. She can operate in the sun, she's unaffected by holy items, hardly ever needs to feed. But she's just a prototype. If I can destroy her, the so-called Orphans will have to start all over. Without their leaders, it will be years before they can begin another project like her."

He turned back to his hammering. "It's the least I can do for Jimmy."

Thomas gnawed on his cheek, trying desperately to think. Was Warrenna really some kind of advanced vampire project like O'Neal said? Did he believe the crazy man bleeding him, or the weirdo who messed with his head?

He shifted his elbow, hoping to tip the needle upward a bit and let gravity slow the bleeding. *Either way, the vampires are my only way out of this. And they're heading straight into a trap.*

Chapter 16

The cool, oily leather of the Volvo's backseat pressed into Warrenna's sunburned cheek, and the powerful air-conditioning soothed the rest of her sore skin. The heavy tint on the windows subdued the landscape from bright desert to dusky highway.

Back to Bascomville. Back to Chiricahua, where the only person I reached out to is now afraid of me.

Warrenna was trying to figure out a way to transfer out of third-hour English when her father's cell phone rang. Richard glanced at the display and raised an eyebrow.

He put the receiver to his ear and said, "How did you get this number?"

After a moment he said, "That is an unacceptable trade." He waited another second and hung up.

Richard clicked on the turn signal and took the next exit off the highway.

Alexandria yawned, looking one way, then the next. "This is the wrong exit, *ámor.*"

"I know." He pulled over into some dirt, moved the gearshift to park, and closed his eyes.

Then he said four words Warrenna would never forget: "Thomas has been kidnapped."

"What?" mother and daughter both cried.

"I heard him. He was in pain." Richard's voice was steady and eerily quiet. "The caller said he would kill Thomas if we didn't exchange Warrenna for him. He knew exactly who we were. It must be a hunter."

Warrenna couldn't make herself breathe. *Oh, Tommy, what did I get you into?*

Alexandria sighed and rubbed her eyes. "It's a trap."

Richard nodded in agreement and stared at the steering wheel.

Her parents' cool reactions sparked anger in Warrenna. "We're not just going to let him die, right?"

"No, hon," Alexandria said. "He's too important. We must try to retrieve him."

Richard's cell phone was at his ear again. He pressed the walkie-talkie button and said, "Vince?"

Beep. "Yah," Uncle Vince's voice came.

"We pulled over on Mescal Road. Meet us there. I just got a call. A hunter has kidnapped Thomas."

Beep. "Damn it! I knew I should have tailed him last night."

"You were busy testing Necole. But we can't think about that now. We need your spell again."

Beep. "I'm coming up on the exit now."

Richard put the phone down and turned to his daughter. "The caller gave me a location to bring you for a trade. We need to see if Thomas is really there, so you and Vince are going to perform his spell again."

"The see-though-Tommy's-eyes trick we did on Saturday?"

"That's the one."

She heard a rumbling behind her, and a look out the back window revealed Aunt Tammy's approaching Explorer. The wheels were still rolling when Uncle Vince's lanky form hopped out of the passenger door and jogged to the Volvo.

He quickly slid inside opposite Warrenna and slammed the door. "You got the book, Renny?"

"Book? Oh, ah—yes," Warrenna said, remembering. She placed the journal between them. "Take me with you again."

Uncle Vince glanced at her parents, then back at Warrenna. "You probably don't want to see what's happening to him."

Alexandria shook her head. "She will see more than you could, Vincent. We're certain of that. And we need as much information as we can get."

Uncle Vince shrugged and turned back to Warrenna. "Since I'm doing this on the fly, you're only going to get a couple of seconds. Look around as much as you can."

Warrenna nodded, and Uncle Vince took a deep breath and closed his eyes. He extended his hands, and Warrenna placed her palms on his.

The hollow warmth advanced up her arms as she waited for him to open his eyes.

He took another breath, and his lids parted. Deep blue static consumed Warrenna's sight.

She was in a dim room, surrounded by dusty church pews and spray-painted initials. *Coyotes 4Life* was etched into a nearby wall.

She smelled blood.

The bitter, wonderful scent pervaded everything and pulled her sight downward.

A tube extended from someone's arm, dropping into a bucket.

A bucket half-full of the most mouthwatering blood she ever smelled.

She wanted to bring the bucket to her lips, to gulp down all that life, to feel the warmth spill down her chin, dribble down her neck as she filled herself with sustenance, with power.

* * *

"Renna!"

With a jarring flash, Warrenna was back in the Volvo. She could see her mother's clenched, crimson-colored face above the passenger seat.

Something restrained Warrenna's shoulders, but the smell of blood flowed through her, calling to her to feed.

That is the scent! We must have that blood! It will make us strong!

Then she remembered whose blood the bucket held, whose life she wanted to bathe in.

No! We must help Tommy, not hurt him.

Her talons and fangs gradually retracted, and the world lost its crimson hue. Then she began to shiver, tears running unchecked down her cheeks. "So much blood," she gasped.

Richard released his grip on her shoulders. "Tell us what you saw, Renna."

Warrenna sniffled and tried to remember. "A small room with dirty pews. There was spray-paint and cigarette burns everywhere. *Coyotes 4 Life* was carved on a wall. And blood. So much blood."

The craving churned inside her. Her jaw and fingers ached. *Evil Renny doesn't like to be teased.*

It took all her will to silence the voice.

"That's the Mission," Uncle Vince said. "I remember it from high school. Damn. There's no shade for miles around it."

Alexandria nodded. "Then I suppose we'll have to make our own."

Richard turned to Vince. "What do you say? How long could Tamara give us?"

Uncle Vince rubbed his head and frowned. "If things go well, maybe a minute. Maybe."

Richard nodded. "Then we'll have to work quickly." He

clicked the gearshift into drive. "Go tell Tamara to meet us at the Connolly Ranch Road turn-off from Carter Avenue. Top speed. And Vince?"

"Yeah?"

"Thanks."

Uncle Vince grinned, said "Whatever," and hurried out of the car.

Richard slammed his foot on the accelerator, spinning the tires and kicking up a cloud of dust. In a couple of heartbeats, the Volvo was back on the highway traveling at one hundred miles per hour.

Warrenna found her seat belt and strapped herself in. "Mom, what did you mean, make our own shade?"

"I'll explain in a minute, Renna." Alexandria looked to her husband. "We should call in the cavalry, love. There are fifteen Orphans in Maldecido who will come if we say the word."

He shook his head. "There's no time. It would take them an hour just to get here, and judging from Renna's reaction, Thomas doesn't have that long. We'll have to do this ourselves."

"Are you crazy?" Alexandria faltered. "It's a trap. We know it's a trap."

"I know, *corazón.*" Richard smiled at his wife. "We'll just have to break through it."

Alexandria's mouth hung open for a moment. But then she bit her lip and took her husband's free hand into hers. She turned to their daughter. "Listen to me very carefully, Renna. Aunt Tammy can make the sky dark during the day. She needs Uncle Vince to do it, and it's extremely demanding on both of them. They'll keep it up as long as they can, but then they'll both drop from exhaustion. We need you right beside them."

"Why?"

"So when they finish, you can cover Aunt Tammy with a reflective blanket. It will only be dark for a minute."

"So where will you be?"

Richard slowed down to turn onto the Carter Avenue exit, then nailed the gas again.

"Your father and I will rush into the Mission as soon as the darkness allows us. We'll grab Thomas and get him back to the car as fast as we can."

"Which means we'll be in our other forms," Richard added. "We might be a little scary-looking."

The prospect of seeing both of her parents as hideous beasts was unsettling enough to Warrenna. But then she remembered Alexandria's difficulty walking after her last cleansing. "Can you handle a transformation, Mom?"

"I'll be fine," Alexandria said, but her eyes wouldn't meet Warrenna's.

"Hang on," Richard said, and slammed on the brakes and skidded onto a dirt road to the right. After fifty feet or so, the car came to an abrupt stop, and Richard turned his head to look for Tamara's Explorer. His eyes were cool and grim.

After a couple of anxious seconds, the black SUV fishtailed onto the dirt behind them. Richard's cell phone beeped.

Uncle Vince's voice came. "See that hill up there? the Mission is just around it."

"Roger," Richard said into his phone. "We'll approach it slowly and park before the curve."

Beep. "Got it."

They recommenced down the dirt road, slowly, so that the vehicles barely kicked up any dust. "Here's the plan, Renna," Richard began. "You're going to climb that hill with Uncle Vince and Aunt Tammy. You'll shade Aunt Tammy the whole way with an umbrella. When you reach the top, they'll start their spell. You need to keep Aunt Tammy shaded and watch the Mission."

"What am I watching for?"

Richard gnawed on his lower lip for a moment. "Anything we haven't thought of. Maybe this hunter doesn't work alone.

Maybe he'll make a run for it once your mother and I arrive. You need to communicate whatever you see to Uncle Vince and Aunt Tammy. They'll be too busy to notice anything, so you'll have to."

Warrenna nodded, and Richard continued. "Once the spell wears off, they'll both collapse. Cover Aunt Tammy with the blanket, then wait for Uncle Vince to wake up to help you carry her back to the Explorer. But if you see anything coming toward you, you toss that blanket on your aunt and get out of there."

"Okay." Warrenna said. "So you two have to make it to the Mission, get Thomas, and make it back to the car before the darkness wears off."

Alexandria nodded. "The distances won't be the problem. Springing the hunter's trap will delay us the most."

Richard brought the car to a slow stop at the foot of the hill. Her parents looked at each other for a moment, then turned to her.

"Renna," Alexandria said, "we'll leave the keys in the ignition. If something goes wrong and we don't come out of there, get back to the car and go. Call the police on your cell phone and tell them you saw something out by Connolly Ranch Road, like a brush fire, or some undocumented aliens. Whatever you like. Then drive to Maldecido. The Orphans will take care of you."

Warrenna's jaw dropped. "I can't just leave you."

Alexandria raised a slender hand and shushed her. "Honey, if we can't save Thomas's life, then no one can. If you go in there after us, you'll certainly be destroyed. Losing Thomas, as terrible as it would be, is something the Orphans can survive. Losing your father and me is something the Orphans can survive. But you must live through this. If the Orphans lose you, then they lose hope. And if they lose hope, the beast will overtake them. All our years of fighting will have been for naught."

The idea of life without her parents hit Warrenna like a fist to the stomach. "You guys can't die," she choked.

Richard smiled, and his grim eyes softened for a moment. He

reached over the seat and took Warrenna's small hand into his firm grip. "I know you will make us proud. Hell, you already have."

He held the gaze and brought the cell phone up to his lips. "Climb up to the top of the hill. Warrenna will shade Tamara as the two of you bring the darkness."

Beep. "We're ready when you are."

Warrenna looked her parents' smiling faces. *I can't lose them. I can't go on alone!*

"Just don't die, all right? I'll see you back here."

The sun shone hot on Warrenna's face and hands as she strode through the dirt toward the Explorer. *This is insane. A week ago, all I worried about was my own pointless existence. Now an angel that I accidentally enthralled is bleeding to death a few hundred feet from me, and my parents might get killed trying to rescue him. And it's all because of me. Why couldn't I keep my suffering to myself?*

Uncle Vince stepped out of the truck and gestured for her to follow him around to the rear. From the back, he retrieved a tall black umbrella and a shiny blanket that hurt Warrenna's sun-sensitive eyes to look at.

She extended the umbrella, tucked the blanket under her other arm, and went around to the passenger door to help Aunt Tammy out of the truck.

"It'll be okay," Aunt Tammy said as she stepped out of the vehicle. "Your parents have seen many battles. They can survive anything."

Warrenna nodded, but she wondered if her mother and father looked so worried before every battle. Now was not the time to ask, though.

Climbing the hill while keeping Aunt Tammy out of the sun was slow and tricky. Warrenna had to watch her footing amongst the desert brush and steady the umbrella's shadow at the same time. Uncle Vince wagged his fingers and whispered to himself, ignoring Warrenna and her difficulties. Twice she slipped, and Aunt Tammy gasped in pain. But about halfway up, Warrenna got the hang of it, and they reached the low summit all too soon.

"Don't worry about leaving me under the blanket," Aunt Tammy said. "I once spent an entire day under one of those things. I'll just take a little nap." She gave a reassuring smile. "I'll need one after what I'm about to do."

Warrenna nodded. From this height, she could see the side of a small brownish building just past the foot of the hill, about fifty yards in front of her. A blue sedan with a gray hood was parked a few yards away from the arched entrance. If she craned her neck, she could see her parents' black Volvo behind her.

Warrenna's stomach knotted up, and she gripped the umbrella-handle tightly. *Something awful is about to happen. And I'm going to get a bird's-eye view of it.*

Uncle Vince turned to stand face-to-face with Aunt Tammy, and closed his eyes. Aunt Tammy removed her orange shades and looked to Warrenna, who then saw her doctor's eyes for the very first time.

The irises were bright green. But inside them, or maybe on top of them, were three evenly spaced, bright orange triangles.

"Don't worry," Aunt Tammy said with a wink. "They won't hurt you."

She turned back to Uncle Vince, took his hands in hers, and looked straight up into Warrenna's umbrella.

The air became still, and Aunt Tammy inhaled deeply. After a few seconds she flinched, and a pair of specks emerged from her eyes, like black pollen escaping from a pair of green lilies. The specks twisted upward, curled under the umbrella, and disappeared into the pale sky.

That pair was followed by another pair, and then another, and another, until a pulsing line of curlicues rose from Aunt Tammy's face. The specks coalesced into a thin black cloud that hung like diesel smoke over the Mission and the hill.

Warrenna thought she could hear the buzzing of insects, like gnats, as she watched the darkness stream out of her doctor's eyes. She wondered where exactly all the gnats were coming from. *Maybe Aunt Tammy has her own black marble.*

Aunt Tammy shuddered, and fangs slid down through her clenched teeth. Hooked talons curved around Uncle Vince's fingers, but he didn't move.

"Stay with me, Tammy," he urged. His clenched face strained with effort. "You can do it."

A guttural noise nastier than any dog Warrenna had ever heard escaped from Aunt Tammy's throat, and the stream of black became solid. The cloud quickly darkened, dramatically dimming the area around them. Warrenna could still see bright yellow earth on the horizon, but for the moment, she stood in a patch of moonless twilight.

Aunt Tammy panted, her hips swaying from side to side like an unsteady drunk. Warrenna could see her aunt's pinwheel-like irises constricting beneath half-closed lids.

But then movement near the Volvo caught her attention. She shifted her gaze and saw two blurs moving at incredible speed toward the Mission. About twenty feet before the building, the shapes sprang high into the air, soaring nearly to Warrenna's eye-level. For a half-second, she could make out a couple of humanoid shapes and two pairs of bright red eyes.

Then the shapes plunged into the Mission's roof with a crash. A cloud of plaster chunks and wood splinters flew into the air. A second later, an orange flash erupted from inside the building, and a boarded window blew out in a puff of dust and wood chips.

Warrenna heard a strangled cry of pain, and then another, like snarls of wounded mountain lions.

Aunt Tammy groaned, and both she and Uncle Vince crumpled to the ground. The black cloud vanished, brightening the landscape in the blink of an eye.

No! It's too fast. They're still in there!

Flames burst through the blown-out window. Two loud bangs echoed across the desert.

Warrenna tossed the umbrella aside and threw the blanket over Aunt Tammy's limp form. The world turned crimson.

If my parents and Tommy are gone, then what's left to lose?

She was down the hill and through the front door of the Mission in a heartbeat. She clicked her talons together as she ran, and the voice urged her on. *We will have him!*

The door opened to reveal a man in a familiar white suit. He held a gun. Behind him she saw Thomas, slumped in a chair, with two black holes in his chest.

"NO!" she shrieked, and lunged at the man.

Blinding white light enveloped her.

Every part of Thomas felt tired, from his neck and shoulders down through his legs and toes. Even his eyes felt tired. He was tempted to just drop off to sleep and let this ordeal play itself out without him, but he was afraid he would never wake.

His sight chanced to fall on the tube extending from his side, still dark with traveling blood. He didn't follow the tube to its receptacle, though. He didn't want to get that weird heat in his jaw and wrists again.

Thomas recalled Richard's words. *"Something went to great care to make her bleed for a long time. Whatever did this to her wanted to watch her suffer."*

"How come you don't just kill me now?"

"Because that would be too good for you."

O'Neal's voice came from behind him now. Thomas heard pouring liquid and the clink of glass touching glass, but didn't look to see what his captor was doing.

"You get to die slowly," O'Neal continued. "And when I'm

done with you, there won't be a drop left for the bastards to feed on. I'll leave you a dried-out husk. Like they left my poor Jimmy."

Thomas sighed. "What if these vampires aren't anything like whoever killed your brother? I mean, that had to be fifteen, twenty years ago, right? For all you know, these vampires could have killed whoever killed Jimmy. They could be totally different."

"No vampires are different."

O'Neal grabbed the back of the chair and swung his face to within inches of Thomas's. His beady eyes were bright with anger. "They are all fiends. They'd like nothing better than to exterminate every one of us."

O'Neal's cheeks quivered, and he turned away. "They just left him. They took advantage of Jimmy's kindness, used him up, and left him in the desert to be picked apart by buzzards. Well, now I get to do that to another one of theirs." He glared at Thomas. "Now shut up or I'll gag you."

Thomas chewed on his cheek. Reasoning with the man was obviously out of the question. *Nope, it's up to the vampires, who may or may not have been using me. Fantastic.*

A shadow flickered across the rays of light pouring in from the holes in the ceiling. The rays soon disappeared, leaving the room utterly dark.

He took a slow breath. *What's happening now?*

Something crunched above him, like a wrecking ball crashing into a brick house. Sawdust shot up his nose and into his mouth.

He blinked away some grit, and found a pair of red eyes floating to his left.

A triangle of flame flew through the air from behind him, shattering with a tinkle of glass. Flames exploded around the floating eyes, illuminating the room. Thomas could make out a human shape spinning in a sickening dance of pain and heat. The shape dropped to the ground and rolled about in a ball of light, but the thrashes and slaps did nothing to keep the flames from devouring its flesh.

A snarl turned Thomas's head. O'Neal was holding a wooden baseball bat, fending off another humanoid creature with jabs and prods. The beast's angry red eyes glowed in the orange firelight. Its shoulders were hunched like a lion about to pounce.

The monster darted toward O'Neal in a blur of speed, knocking the bat away like it was a chopstick. Then it swung a handful of hooked claws at the hunter. O'Neal stumbled backward, but the vampire advanced, grasping his white lapels with both bony paws.

But then the beast yelped and recoiled. It waved its hands about as though trying to shake something sticky off its fingers.

"Holy garment," Thomas mumbled, understanding.

O'Neal quickly retrieved his baseball bat and confidently stepped forward to take a mighty swing at the monster's head.

"This is for Jimmy!" he yelled, and he connected with a nauseating crunch.

The beast staggered back, and O'Neal rammed the bat into its breastbone, which sent the thing crashing through the pew just in front of Thomas.

That was when Thomas noticed the vampire's hair, which was long and reddish-brown, like Alexandria's. That meant the one rolling around in the corner was probably Richard.

O'Neal doused Alexandria's gasping form with liquid from a plastic bottle that he quickly threw away. Then he held out a grill-lighter and clicked the trigger.

Alexandria erupted in flame. She rolled about in a pitiful attempt to put out the fire, but it did her no good, just as Richard's frantic spins had done nothing but spread the fire around his body.

Both vampires roared, filling the room with throaty cries of torture.

The wails echoed again and again in Thomas's ears. His body glowed with warmth from deep inside his chest. *Pain. Too much pain.*

O'Neal passed in front of Thomas, carrying his black briefcase. "Lots of ways to kill a vampire, m'boy, but I like fire the best. You see, it's the most painful over the longest period of time."

He looked at his watch. "I'd love to stick around, but I think I'll go before the cavalry arrives. I hope you get to enjoy their deaths before you die."

I must relieve their pain. They're suffering because of me. His eyes rolled back in his head.

O'Neal jumped back. "Mother of God, you're glowing! I knew you were some kind of demon."

Two deafening reports brought Thomas's sight back. O'Neal stood in front of the now-open door. Bright sunlight washed over the smoky room.

The old man was holding a pistol, and the pistol was pointed at Thomas.

"NO!" a familiar voice shrieked.

Thomas bowed his head to find two black holes in the right side of his chest.

Blinding white light enveloped his vision, except for his chest, where the holes had joined together and were slowly expanding in every direction.

Chapter 17

The hole pulsed with swirls of purple and black. Eyes-of-Dawn-Sky pictured the evil spirit as an invisible tick, sucking his life away from inside his thigh.

The darkness held his eyes, and speckled his vision when he finally looked up at the fiery sunset. Orange light washed over the desert, and the air was still, like the mountain was waiting for him to do what he came to do.

He threw the knife to the ground. "No."

Turning on his heel, Eyes-of-Dawn-Sky strode down the dusty mountain. He knew now. There was another way to expel the evil spirit. He would keep it from ever entering him.

He approached the woman with the long black braid. Tears ran down her thin cheeks.

"Don't cry, Mother-to-Doves," he said. "I'm not going to die."

She gasped, but Eyes-of-Dawn-Sky didn't look back.

He took another step, and sank into water up to his knees. He stood in a clear stream. The cool current stung his wound. White, leafless trees clawed at the noonday sky around him.

Mother-to-Doves stood in front of him. Her dark eyes were serious. "You're going the wrong way."

"No." He moved her aside with a powerful arm. The clear water turned blood-red.

"I'm not going to die."

The water thickened with each step as he waded down the stream. When he could finally move no further, he saw that the red water had become yellow sand. He lifted his legs, climbing out onto the surface on his knees.

Mother-to-Doves stood over him, offering her hand. "You cannot do this. You will be lost. We must return to the stream, and then to the peak of Zeraphet."

He stood on his own. "I know where I am going. I have to make this right."

After a few steps down the sandy hill, his vision blurred, and the tanned tents bearing the mark of the mid-flight arrow appeared before him. He saw no one as he passed in and out of the long scarlet shadows.

The medicine man waited inside his tent. Eyes-of-Dawn-Sky pulled the red feather from his hair and held it out to the old man. "I am not going to die," he said. "I am going back. I will fix this."

Wisdom-of-Elk did not take the feather. He closed his eyes. "You are going the wrong way, warrior. You cannot change what has already come."

Eyes-of-Dawn-Sky threw the feather to the ground, where it shattered to red dust. "It is already changed!"

The flap of the tent opened onto the battlefield. Men were all around, firing bows, swinging hatchets, grappling, falling. White war-paint and blood blended into pink puddles along the rocky ground.

An enemy warrior was upon Eyes-of-Dawn-Sky, swinging a knife at his face. But Eyes-of-Dawn-Sky did not retreat. Knowing the swing would suddenly dip to his leg, he reached out and caught his enemy's wrist.

"I am not going to die!" Eyes-of-Dawn-Sky cried, and he wrenched his grip.

His opponent's dark eyes never changed expression, but the knife dropped to the ground.

"Thomas!"

Eyes-of-Dawn-Sky blinked. That was Mother-to-Doves's voice. Why was she on the battlefield?

Men froze in place; arrows hovered in mid-flight. The scene was still, save for a blood-red cloud bubbling in the pale sky.

Mother-to-Doves stood beside him. "Thomas, please go back to the cliff. You'll be lost forever if you don't."

There was something familiar about that strange name. Eyes-of-Dawn-Sky picked up the poisoned blade that had brought about the end of his life. "I am not supposed to die. I'm not ready."

"You're right, Thomas. But you should be fighting for *your* life, not the warrior's. Let him return to the land."

The red cloud rolled across the horizon, as though an arrow had pierced the sky and the blood of the heavens was spilling down to the earth. Eyes-of-Dawn-Sky could see the distant tree line fading to a crimson stain as the color advanced toward the battlefield.

The name felt important. His lips formed the word: "Thomas."

As he said the word, Mother-to-Dove's braid slowly retreated into her scalp. She bobbed her head, and her hair lightened from black to auburn. Her skin paled to white, and her dark eyes turned gray.

"Warrenna?"

Eyes-of-Dawn-Sky didn't know where the name came from. His eyes tingled and pleasant warmth grew in his chest. The girl nodded, and her eyes flashed a familiar red.

After a second of confusion, Thomas understood. He was *inside* the warrior. He had forgotten who he was, and was trying to save the wrong life. Thomas couldn't remember why his life needed saving, but he knew he wasn't supposed to go the wrong way in the dream. Doing that brought the red cloud, and the red cloud ended everything it touched.

Thomas quickly closed his eyes and pictured the sunset. When he opened them, he was again standing on the edge of the holy cliff. The red was nowhere to be seen.

The dagger was at his chest again. But Thomas wondered what would happen to him once he shattered the ice in the warrior's heart. Eyes-of-Dawn-Sky would return to the land, but where would *he* go? How would he save his own life?

He didn't know. But giving the warrior peace felt like the right thing to do.

Eyes-of-Dawn-Sky plunged the knife into his heart, and Thomas's vision flooded with white.

Am I dead?

White was all around him, but Thomas could see his blurry hands waving as though he stood in a mist. His t-shirt looked like a bottle of black ink had been dumped down the right side of his chest.

He thought he could hear the static of a badly tuned radio in the distance. As the noise grew steadily louder, Thomas realized that it was actually composed of thousands of voices, murmuring together. The sound was nonsense, the blended prattle of languages he couldn't understand.

But then one voice emerged from the babble:

"Hello, Thomas."

A woman appeared before him. Her tall body consisted of a long black dress dotted with tiny crimson hourglasses. The dress didn't really end. It just faded downward until the mist overwhelmed it.

A black hourglass hovered above her right hand. She waved her fingers, and the hourglass turned onto its side. The voices ceased their confusing racket.

"You made it back," the woman said. Her voice was deep and soothing, like a cellist's dirge. "That's impressive. This is a difficult place to navigate, for most people."

Thomas remembered a voice calling his name, leading him back to the cliff. "I think I had some help."

She nodded. Her white face was impossibly smooth, and Thomas thought he might be looking at caryatid statue from ancient Greece. The black lips moved, but the dark eyes revealed no emotion or intention.

"My daughter," the woman said. "She seems to care about you quite a lot."

"Warrenna." The name was on his lips without thought. "She found me."

"You don't know how right you are. I didn't think she could do it, but she brought you to me. I'm glad she did. I've wanted to talk to you for some time."

"Daughter...?" Thomas struggled, then understood. He wondered if he should fall to his knees, or look away from her eyes out of respect. But in the end he just stared. "You must be Zera, then."

"Very perceptive, Thomas. You're a difficult man to track down. You traipse through the dreams of others without hesitation, as though it were the most natural thing in the world."

Thomas squinted. The smell of ground black pepper flared in his nostrils, which just confused him more. "Aren't they my dreams?"

Zera raised a black eyebrow. "I guess it would be difficult for you to tell. No, you're what I call a *Traveler*. You stay with one person's dream for a few nights, then you jump to another's." Her dark eyes twinkled. "Sometimes these dreamers have been dead for centuries. Yet that doesn't stop you from haunting their dreamt-up scenes."

Thomas gripped his forehead. Was this really Zera? And how could he spend time in a dead person's dream? "So I'm a Traveler," he said, trying out the title. "Is Warrenna a Traveler, too?"

A ripple moved through Zera's sable hair as she nodded. "Her abilities aren't nearly as refined as yours. You move about in this other realm as though you've been Traveling for a long, long time. But you and I both know there's more happening with you."

Zera turned and took a few paces as she spoke. The hourglass hovered alongside her. "Not long ago I saw you killing spiders inside an Orphan's nightmare. You ended up curing a great deal of her curse, extending her life by several years. That's not something a Traveler or anyone else should be able to do. But you did. I've never seen anything like it."

He stared into the bright white nothingness. "I don't know what to tell you. I thought maybe I was an angel."

Zera chuckled, a stuttering violin. "No, Thomas. Angels can't travel between dreams. And angels certainly can't cure the curse. No, you must be something else."

Thomas's knees turned to pudding. *First she tells me I hang out in the dreams of dead people, then she tells me I can cure the curse, but I'm not an angel.*

He wrinkled his nose. And what was with that ground black pepper odor? It was making him nauseous, but the scent was familiar.

"That odor," Thomas mumbled. "That's you, isn't it?"

Zera blinked. Her dress glowed deep crimson for a moment. "Me?"

He was on to something. He could feel it. "The pepper. I smelled it after I blacked out, and when I freaked out on Mariah. That was you. You were there."

Zera's jaw dropped. "Ah, well, I'm not going to lie to you,

Thomas. I was trying to communicate with you while you were waking, but it didn't work, and you ended up losing a bit of your memory. And when you were with that other girl, I was trying to remind you of your link with my daughter. I'm afraid my reminder was a bit too strong. I didn't intend for you to react so powerfully."

Thomas straightened. *So Warrenna didn't enthrall me. It was just this lady messing with my head.*

The idea of catching a goddess off-guard emboldened him. "So, you can just dive into anybody's head and give them suggestions?"

She smiled again. "No. Besides my Orphans, the only humans I can communicate with are Travelers. But I only have a scent when I'm dealing with creatures I am related to."

His stomach fluttered. "Related to?"

She nodded. "But I didn't create you like I did my daughter. Someone else did." She tapped her perfect chin. "Funny, I thought all my brothers and sisters were gone. I wonder which one of them made you." She shrugged. "The answers will come with time. I am glad you were made, though. You are going to help to me quite a bit. Assuming you live, of course."

"Of course." Thomas wondered how much of this confusing conversation he was going to remember if he survived the return trip. "Warrenna didn't enthrall me," he whispered, hoping the idea would somehow stick

Thinking about Warrenna reminded him of something. "As long as I'm here, can I ask you something else?"

"I suppose that's fair, after all you've been through. You may ask."

"Why did you make it so Warrenna would be born cursed? It seems kind of…"

"Cruel?"

Thomas nodded. "A little."

Zera cocked her head. Pinpricks of light swirled in her dark eyes, fireflies darting in an onyx field. "It would take more time than we have here to explain. But just between you and me, I will say this. I made Warrenna the way she is because my people needed a leader."

Thomas pursed his lips. "I see."

She smiled. "I doubt it. But now it is time to go. I really do hope you survive the rest of your journey."

"Thanks."

"See you next time, Thomas."

"Wait, next time? What does that mean?"

The hourglass turned, and Zera's form faded away. The babbling voices returned, but quickly went silent.

In a blink, the white around him turned orange. Roaring fire replaced the voices. A man in a white suit held a pistol in his hand. His beady blue eyes gleamed with hatred.

The cause of the pain.

The vampire-hunter fired his gun, but the bullets passed through Thomas as though he weren't there.

Thomas extended his arm of white flame. O'Neal's eyes widened and his mouth opened, but he made no sound as Thomas held his flame to the hunter's neck.

And then everything went black.

Chapter 18

Steady waves crashed in Warrenna's ears. The pleasant roar reminded her of Corriander Beach, but she knew she was far too warm to be lying near the Washington coastline.

Her cheeks stung with the familiar pressure of sunlight, and she instinctively raised her hand to shield her eyes. But why should she be afraid of the sun?

Then she remembered the curse. Her growling stomach and the ache in her jaw reminded her that she just transformed. But the marble gleamed so brightly that even imagining it was painful. Evil Renny felt far away, like she slumbered in a white cocoon.

But why did she unchain the beast in the first place? She remembered asking Thomas to return to a cliff where an amazing sunset was taking place.

Her eyes blinked open, and she recognized the entry-arch of the Mission above her.

Thomas.

The sunset and the cliff evaporated from memory as she scrambled to her feet and into the shade of the Mission.

She was almost beaten back by the overpowering smell of blood. Her sinuses burned with it. Her heart pounded and her eyes watered. Just before her vision blurred, she saw Thomas's form slumped in a chair in front of some of the pews. To his left sat a shiny, familiar bucket.

She recalled the vision she had in the Volvo, and her mouth filled with saliva at the thought of all that blood.

No. She took a step forward. *I must help him, not drain him.*

Something crunched under her foot. Warrenna looked down to see a blackened skeleton with its hands wrapped around its neck. A silver pistol and a charred briefcase lay by its hip.

Warrenna stared at the bones for a moment, fascinated by the horrid pose. *Can't say I'm sorry to see that guy fricasseed.* She ripped her gaze away and moved to Thomas.

When she was close enough to see him clearly, she gasped. His skin was white as milk, and the right side of his t-shirt was black with dried blood. A thick rope ran across his belly, binding him to the chair. A glance revealed more ropes around his shins. His arms were pinned behind him, his chin rested against his chest, and his eyes were closed. She couldn't tell if he was breathing.

Her throat tightened. Was she too late?

She gingerly put her hand over Thomas's heart. The beat was soft and quick. "Tommy, can you hear me?"

His eyes fluttered open, but he looked past her and gurgled. A dark stream of blood erupted from his mouth and snaked down his pale neck, disappearing into the stain on his t-shirt. His eyes rolled back, and he went limp again.

"Okay Tommy," she said, trying to sound calm. "Don't worry, I'm gonna get you out of here."

She tried to untie the rope around his stomach, but the knot was tight, and her aching fingers quivered. She bit her lip. "Okay Tommy, no big deal. I'll just drag you."

She pulled on the back of the chair until it tipped into her hands. But she could barely sustain his weight at a standstill. Dragging him would be impossible.

Panic squeezed her lungs. *What do I do now? Does he just die in front of me?*

"Okay, Tommy," she said, her voice trembling, "I need some help. I'm going to go get Uncle Vince. He's the only one here that won't burn up in the sun. I'll be right back, I promise."

"Drink from him."

Warrenna turned to find a mass of stakes and splinters before her, as though an anvil had fallen upon the pew from a great height. Curled on what remained of the bench was Alexandria.

Most of her mother's clothing was gone, and the scraps that remained were but fringed tatters around her legs. Huge blisters dotted her right cheek, right arm, and both hands, which she held lifelessly before her. Her fingers were melted together and covered with soot.

"Oh, God, Mom!"

Warrenna was nauseous with guilt. *I was so worried about Thomas, I didn't even think about my parents!*

"Don't worry about us," Alexandria whispered. The right side of her lips remained sealed as she spoke. "Whatever Thomas did to incinerate the hunter also put out the fires consuming your father and me. We are badly hurt, but Thomas is dying. You have to help him, now."

Warrenna looked up for a second and found a mass of flesh huddled in the opposite corner. A moment's concentration revealed a pair of hazel eyes looking her way.

The eyes belonged to her father. But all of Richard's hair was gone. Even his eyebrows and goatee had burnt off.

"Renna," Alexandria's voice came. "Uncle Vince will be unconscious for several minutes. You must drink from the bucket. It will give you the strength to do what you have to do."

Warrenna stole a glance at the pail and all the delicious blood it held. "But what if I lose control? I'll enthrall him again. I might even kill him!"

"You said you didn't harm him the first time," Alexandria wheezed. "You must risk it, Renna. Otherwise, Thomas will certainly die."

Warrenna remembered that night in Tebon Canyon when she wanted to scare Thomas away. She put forth all the evil she had inside her for him to see, and he wasn't scared. He said he knew she would never hurt him.

Warrenna approached the silver pail, breathing so hard that spittle bubbled to her lips. The plastic hose from her vision stood in the bucket like a child's twisty-straw.

"Mom, Dad, I promise I'll come back for you."

She brought the bucket to her lips. *I hope you were right about me, Tommy.*

Lukewarm blood filled her mouth, and her eyes shot open on the first swallow. Lightning flowed through every muscle as her talons and fangs slid into place. She kept drinking. She inhaled blood into her eager lungs, the sweet nectar dripped down her chin and tickled her neck, and still she drank.

Her mind woke. She heard her parents' concerns about how far this dose of blood would set their daughter back. She heard Aunt Tammy's worries about the noises coming from the Mission, and how she hoped Uncle Vince would lie next to her forever.

But she could also feel Thomas drowning in pain and confusion. He was not made to breathe blood.

Warrenna released the empty pail, and her talons sliced through each of Thomas's bonds before the bucket hit the ground. She lifted him in her arms like he was a child, and placed her mouth over the wound in his chest. His was the best blood there ever was, and what remained in his shell could make her even faster, even more aware. He could sustain her for weeks.

But then Thomas gasped, the air shimmered, and she pulled her jaws from his chest.

No. This one must live. He can make more blood alive than dead.

She reached the Volvo in two strides, where she gently laid Thomas across the backseat, face up. Then she jumped behind the wheel.

Turning the ignition with her talons proved difficult, but she managed. She knew she could run to a hospital faster than the machine could carry her, but she would certainly be seen doing so. The humans would then be wary of her, and that would make them harder to hunt. And perhaps she would encounter another one like the foolish man in the white suit.

She slammed her foot down on the gas. The wheels spun out, and the vehicle rumbled down the dirt road. The boy would be dead very soon. She doubted she could make it to help in time.

Oh, well. If he dies, no sense in letting all that blood go to waste.

Suddenly he coughed, spraying a fine mist of blood into the air. "Renna?" he gasped, but his eyes didn't open.

"Yeah, baby. I'm right here."

"You found me."

"Don't talk. Just keep breathing."

He burbled, and more fluid erupted from his mouth. His eyes stayed closed. "Renna, I killed O'Neal. I don't know how I did it. I'm not human."

"I know it, baby. Neither am I."

She glanced back at him, and found his eyes wide open, glowing a radiant blue in her singular crimson vision.

"Oh, Renna." His voice was cool as mountain air. "You're so much prettier in your human form."

Then his eyes closed, and his head lolled back into the seat.

A familiar tingly feeling stirred in Warrenna's chest. Then pain sliced through her hands and jaw as her claws and fangs retracted.

Her vision returned to its multicolor palette as the crimson quickly washed away. The Volvo was drifting, so she grabbed at the wheel; she overcorrected, and the vehicle swerved back toward the left lane. Finally she hit the brakes hard enough to stop, but not before she ended up on the opposite shoulder, facing the way she came from.

Warrenna's heart pounded, and her breath came in shallow gasps. She hugged herself to control the shivers. *Was that really me just now? A demon? A monster? Did I really almost kill my friend?*

She pictured the imaginary marble inside her. It was the size of an orange, black as coal, throbbing. But tiny bolts of blue lightning arced within it, contracting it, shrinking it.

Tommy. Even in my other form, he wasn't afraid of me.

She looked at the backseat. Thomas was a mess of blood and torn clothing, and his chest wasn't rising or falling with breath. *Maybe I did kill him.*

Stomach sinking, she turned the car back onto the road, heading east toward town again. She glanced down at her soot-and-blood-smeared clothes, dreading the questions that would surely come when she got him to the hospital. Tears stung her eyes and plunged her vision underwater.

"God, Tommy, I'm sorry!" she wailed. "I shouldn't have asked you to come to Maldecido. I shouldn't have told you I was dangerous to be around. If I'd just kept my mouth shut, my parents wouldn't be hurt and you wouldn't be dying."

Her gray eyes in the rearview mirror said it all: *it's your fault. All of this is your fault.*

"I know!" she yelled at herself. "I didn't ask to be born cursed." She slapped at her reflection, and the mirror tilted to show Thomas's pale, bloody body.

And then she made a decision. *Yeah, I didn't ask to be born this way. But he didn't ask to be shot, either. I can do something about that.*

She took a deep breath and floored the accelerator. Her hands gripped the steering wheel as she guided the Volvo through the desert.

Chapter IY

Warrenna turned in her cloud, watching her hands grow fuzzy as she moved them away from her face. The crash of the waterfall echoed somewhere far away.

She took a deep breath. The ground black pepper-odor was strong.

"Daughter."

Zera's dark features appeared in the blankness. She was smiling.

"It is good to see you when you are not in pain, daughter."

Warrenna stared hard at Zera's inky eyes. "My name is Warrenna. I'd like you to call me that. If we're going to be part of each other's lives, then that's the way it has to be."

Zera raised a dark eyebrow, then nodded. "It is a good name, isn't it? Very well, Warrenna. What can I do for you?"

Warrenna smiled. "I've got a little list."

* * *

"When the Clippers missed, which was nine times in their first ten attempts, they didn't get back on defense fast enough against the up-tempo Kings, who scored easy basket after easy basket. Imagine that."

Thomas's chest ached with each slow breath. He tried to roll over, but his legs wouldn't move. After a second of panic, he realized that most of his body was wrapped in thin sheets.

He blinked, but his vision was one big blur of light. He knew the voice reporting the basketball story, but couldn't place it.

His focus gradually sharpened. Sunlight from a large window bathed his covered legs. Someone sat in front of the window with a newspaper wide open, concealing her face.

Thomas tried to say hello to the familiar-sounding woman, but his throat was raw and swollen, preventing him from making anything but a quiet gasping noise.

That was when he felt the plastic tube running up his right nostril.

I'm hurt. The low mechanical drone behind the woman's steady voice told him he was in a hospital.

Then Thomas remembered a dark, dusty building that stank of beer and cigarettes. There was a man with beady blue eyes pointing a gun while an inferno raged around him. And then tremendous pain in his chest

A conversation with a black-eyed woman holding an hourglass. *Warrenna didn't enthrall me.*

And he remembered Warrenna's fierce, gleaming red eyes in the driver's seat of a car, and her surprised face when he brought back her human form.

I changed her back? How could I have done something like that?

The woman sitting by the window sighed and turned a page.

"Okay, NHL time. Ottawa takes game one from Philadelphia. The Senators usually rely on their potent offense to win games, but Tuesday night it was their defense that brought about a tense game one victory against the visiting Flyers."

No matter how he tried, he couldn't speak. So he snapped his fingers instead.

The woman gasped. "Tommy?"

Peeking over half of the newspaper were the surprised chocolate-brown eyes of Carla, Thomas's older sister.

He smiled and managed to wave his right hand.

Carla threw the paper aside and rushed to the head of the bed. "Hey, you're awake. Welcome back."

He pointed at his throat to ask why he couldn't talk.

Carla touched his hand and wiped away a tear with the sleeve of her green U of Oregon sweatshirt. "You really had us going there." She caught herself, then babbled, "Oh, I don't know how much you remember. You're in Maldecido General, been here for a few days. Someone brought you to the hospital in Bascomville. But we can worry about the details later. There's a tube in your throat right now, but the doctor said they'd remove it as soon as you woke up."

She stopped herself again. "I need to go get Mom and Dad, okay? They're in the waiting room down the hall, I'll be right back."

He smiled and gave her a thumbs-up sign. At that point, he was glad he couldn't speak. How would he explain the scene at the Mission? Or really, anything about why he was there?

A splash of pink on his left caught his attention. A paper cherry blossom hung in a thin glass vase alongside a stack of get-well cards and some balloons tied to a stuffed teddy bear. The cherry blossom was handmade, intricately folded. Thomas could make out a fancy calligraphic *T* drawn on one of the blossom's paper petals.

He extended his left hand, which sent a lightning bolt of pain through his chest. He managed to pluck the pink flower from its vase before collapsing back to the pillow.

His lethargic fingers rubbed the hard points of the petals. On a whim, he pulled on the *T,* and the flower quickly unfolded, spreading out to three wrinkled sheets of paper. The middle sheet contained some writing.

Tommy,

I can't express how sorry I am, and I can't imagine the pain you've gone through at the hands of the hunter. That pain was caused by me, by what I am. And while I can't do anything about how I was born, I've come to realize that I *can* do something about what happens to me and to the people I care about.

I have a gift for you. It's something no one ever gave to me, but something that I can give to you—a choice.

You can have your old life back, the one where there's no such thing as vampires.

I have accepted the responsibility of leading the Orphans while my parents recover, and I can forbid all of my people from seeking you out. It's the least I can do for causing you so much pain. You'll only have your memories to deal with.

You can go back to your family, your friends, school, and basketball, everything that made life wonderful before you met me. Go back to enjoying your youth. Forget about everything that happened in this strange week. Be normal. Blessedly, innocently normal.

You may be the cure for the curse, Tommy Gelbaugh. But if being cured means destroying your life, I'd rather keep fighting this monster inside me.

Sweet Dreams,
W.

P.S. Zera says hello, and congratulates you on completing your journey. She said you would understand.

P.P.S. I thought you'd like to know that Necole is feeling much better. She thanks you for your "pest control." She also said you would understand.

Carla and his parents could return at any second. He hurriedly folded the note and wedged it under his side.

He knew Warrenna's gift couldn't erase what happened at the Mission. It wouldn't heal the wounds in his chest. It also wouldn't change the fact that he was far more than an ordinary guy who had strange dreams. He had to admit it, though. Returning to a world without vampires, hunters, goddesses and angels sounded great. That world sounded safe.

But as Thomas watched his family enter his hospital room, he realized that world didn't exist. Pretending there was no such thing as vampires was no longer possible. And doing so wouldn't keep his family safe.

That's okay. I don't belong in that world anyway.

He swallowed hard, and gave his excited parents a weak thumbs-up.

Epilogue

Hundreds of students passed by Thomas as they traveled across the Southern Arizona University quad. Most walked, but some rolled along on rollerblades or bicycles. The young men and women were white, black, Hispanic, Asian, Native American. They were tall, short, and everywhere in-between. The sun was bright and hot today, so most of them wore shorts and t-shirts.

Thomas didn't like how many of them frowned as they hurried to their destinations. They weren't enjoying the sunshine, the cool breeze, the soft green grass or the company of their peers.

He adjusted his position on the bench and stretched his arms, careful not to accidentally elbow someone off a bicycle. With his eyes closed, their conversations blended in a pleasing, familiar hum.

"Hey, rise and shine, sleepyhead."

Thomas opened his eyes to see Mariah's smirking face. He picked up the binder resting on the bench beside him. "Hey, lady. You ready?"

She nodded. "What about you? Not short of breath or anything?"

He idly rubbed the scars beneath his collarbone. "Nope, feel great. Thanks for asking."

They joined the stream of walking students. "So how was Anthro?" he asked.

Mariah growled and shook her head. "I swear that teaching assistant hates me. She grilled me on the reading, trying to make me look like I didn't know what I was talking about."

"Well, she's obviously intimidated by attractive women. Aren't you used to that sort of thing by now?"

Mariah rolled her eyes. "That's sweet, but it doesn't really help."

"That's what I'm here for!"

They passed a bright green flyer advertising the upcoming SAU basketball tryouts. "Hey, I forgot to tell you," Thomas said. "I got an e-mail from Brendan this morning. He's coming to Maldecido this weekend."

Mariah's eyes sparkled. "That's great. You should call and get Corwyn down here from Phoenix. We'll paint the town. We could go to The Loft. I don't think either of them ever saw it in our B-Ville days."

Thomas's hip beeped. He stopped and pulled a pager out of the holster clipped to his belt. The digits indicated *317*.

Mariah groaned. "Let me guess. Your SIT buddy again?" SIT stood for Survivors of Induced Trauma, a support group. At least, that's what Thomas had told her.

"Uh, yeah," Thomas mumbled. "Mike's having a rough month."

Anything ending in a seven means they're desperate, and that's the third seven this month.

"Can't he wait an hour?" Mariah said. "We've got class."

Thomas shook his head. "I have to be there for him. I'm lucky. I can't remember most of what my own psycho did to me. But Mike still has really vivid memories of his, uh, ordeal. And being alone is very hard for him. He knows I can understand what he's going through. It's what being in Survivors of Induced Trauma's all about."

Mariah sighed. "I know. It just seems like Mike takes advantage of you. I mean, you barely ever need *him*, right?"

Thomas smirked and rubbed his chest again. "I need him more than you might think. Take good notes for me, and I'll call you tonight, okay?"

"Fine."

Thomas kissed her cheek, and hoped her sulkiness was just an act.

He found his car in the student parking lot and drove north for a few miles, until Mount Maldecido dominated the horizon.

Eventually he reached a guardhouse and a heavy beige gate. "Hey, Luis," he called to the squawk box. "They in the big house?"

"Ah, Tomás," the voice called. *"La curación para la maldición! Sí,* they wait for you *a la mansíon.* Thank you for coming."

"S'no prob-le-mo, amigo."

The fence slowly rolled open and Luis said, "Zera is the way."

Thomas drove to the two-story house at the end of the cul-de-sac and found several cars parked along the street. But the driveway was empty, so he brought the Beatermobile to a stop there.

Warrenna waited for him beneath the extended eave. She wore a stylish black button-up shirt with red pinstripes, and gray pants that matched her eyes.

"Ya know," Thomas said, "my human skin doesn't really need that close parking spot."

She shook her head, and they commenced down the shaded path to the front door. "Anything that gets you to the Orphan faster is a good idea. How are the lungs?"

"They're fine, thanks for asking. How's the craving?"

"Very persistent." Her hungry gaze drifted down his body. "I never should have drunk from you."

For a moment Thomas felt like a blue-eyed mouse trapped by a gunmetal-gray cat. Then he smirked. "Yeah, you definitely should've left me to die in the Mission."

Warrenna smiled and rolled her eyes.

"How are your parents?" Thomas asked.

She pursed her lips as she pulled open the front door. "A little better. Mother is moving her right arm again, and Father's speech is much clearer. The craving is making them uncomfortable, but they're managing. Maybe you could visit them after you see the new Orphan?"

Thomas checked his watch. "I want to make my one-thirty class, so maybe afterwards?"

Warrenna put a hand to her forehead. "I pulled you out of American History, didn't I? I'm sorry this keeps happening, I don't want us to bring down your grades."

Thomas waved his hand. "I'm happy to help."

He smiled. *Between rescuing an Orphan and examining the Continental Congress, I'll take the rescue every time.*

Down the hall, they came across Necole's tall form standing before the open double-doors to the great room. The Orphan smiled serenely as they approached.

"Hello, Thomas," she said cordially, then bowed to Warrenna and said, "My lady."

"Ugh." Warrenna grunted. "Necole, how many times do I have to tell you? I'm not your queen. I'm just holding the fort while my parents recover."

Necole nodded, winked at Thomas, then bowed again. "Whatever you say, my lady."

Then she spun around, announcing into the great room, "Make way, Orphans. For Warrenna and Thomas have arrived."

Warrenna blushed as Necole's rich voice echoed throughout the building. "She really likes to embarrass me," she mumbled to Thomas.

"Really?" Thomas said with a grin. "I hadn't noticed."

After stepping around Necole's flourishes, Thomas saw about a dozen Orphans standing around the familiar bed. Most of the faces were new to him. "Hi, everybody."

"Is that the healer?" a hushed voice asked. A pale redheaded girl sighed and hugged her stunned companion. Another voice whispered, "Thanks be to Zera."

Warrenna glared at Thomas. "You're just eating this up, aren't you."

"Maybe a little." He grinned and playfully touched her shoulder.

He felt a tiny spark in his fingers at the touch, and the familiar warmth inside him fired up again. He breathed deep, winked at Warrenna, and took a few strides toward the bed.

The Orphans parted, and someone whispered, "Am I seeing things, or is he glowing white?"

"Come on, people," Warrenna called. "Let's give our healer a little privacy."

The Orphans reluctantly shuffled out, each of them looking over a shoulder to catch one last glimpse of Thomas, the man who could cure the curse.

"Talk to you later, Tommy," Warrenna said as she closed the double-doors behind her.

Aunt Tammy remained in the great room with him, and playfully elbowed his ribs. "There's real energy between you two, you know."

Thomas blushed. "Yeah, I feel something every time I touch her. Whatever it is, it's happening on some level way beyond my understanding."

She nodded. "There's a lot about this world that we don't understand. We almost never make decisions with all the facts. It's impossible."

Thomas glanced at the marks of Zera encircling him. "That's

true. But I'll tell you one thing. I understand how I feel about Mariah. I've felt it for years. It makes sense to my poor little brain."

Aunt Tammy shrugged. "I'm sure your heart will guide you to where you're meant to be."

Thomas rubbed his chin. *She wants to tell me to quit fighting it, that Renna and I are destined to be together. Well, that may be the case, but my heart's pointing me to Mariah. For now.*

He gave her a reassuring grin. "Don't you worry, Aunt Tammy. I'm not going anywhere."

On the bed lay a thick-chested young man with a gaunt white face and fuzzy brown hair. The warmth spread throughout Thomas, and the air in his lungs turned to silk.

"His name is Art," Aunt Tammy said. "We found him after the raid in Las Vegas. He was all right on the ride down, but he began to turn when we got to the Orphanage. The last cleansing put him in this coma."

Thomas nodded, and reached out to touch the young man's forehead. The warmth extended to his fingertips, and his icy-blue eyes rolled back. "Okay, Art. Let's see if I can't bring you back to us."

His palm touched Art's clammy skin, and then darkness surrounded Thomas. A cry rose up from beneath him.

Ripples silently churned in the darkness under his feet, and familiar bluish-white light reflected back at him. Thomas squinted and saw a human form deep within the black water.

Thomas commanded himself to move, and he dove headfirst into the water.

The black liquid evaporated before it could touch him, so Thomas traveled deeper inside a bubble that extended a foot around him. The flailing body grew closer. Art's eyes were closed, but his mouth was open in a plummeting scream.

At last, Thomas caught up to him, and he wrapped his arm

around Art's wide chest. Art's cries stopped at the touch, and his dark eyes gazed in terror at Thomas's glowing form.

"You don't have to be afraid," Thomas said. "I'm here to take you away from this place."

Tears filled Art's eyes as the dark water retreated from his face.

"No, you're not dead," Thomas assured him. "You're going to live again. It will be a difficult life, but it will be your own."

Thomas moved upward, carrying Art toward a bright white light above the water.

They broke the surface, and the white surrounded them.

"Thank you," Art gasped.

Thomas smiled. "No problem. It's what I'm here for."

~END~

About the Author

Patrick Vaughn was raised in Sierra Vista, Arizona, graduated from Northern Arizona University in Flagstaff and now lives in Phoenix. He has been writing his unusual vampire stories for seventeen years and does not plan to stop. He works at a library for blind children and is writing the sequel to The Cure for the Curse. He can be reached at pjv@tangledstream.net or at zerasorphans.com.